Molly Jong-Fast

Molly Jong-Fast is the daughter and grand-daughter of
distinguished writers: writing is in her blood.
She lives in Manhattan.

SCEPTRE

Normal Girl

MOLLY JONG-FAST

SCEPTRE

Copyright © 2000 Molly Jong-Fast

First published in 2000 by Hodder & Stoughton
First published in paperback in 2001 by Hodder & Stoughton
A division of Hodder Headline
A Sceptre Paperback

The right of Molly Jong-Fast to be identified as the Author of
the Work has been asserted by her in accordance with the
Copyright, Designs and Patents Act 1988.

10 9 8 7 6 5 4 3 2 1

A CIP catalogue record for this book is available from the
British Library.

ISBN 0 340 74811 7

Printed and bound in Great Britain
by Clays Ltd, St Ives plc

Hodder & Stoughton
A division of Hodder Headline
338 Euston Road
London NW1 3BH

This book is dedicated to my grandma, Bettie Fast, who gave me a thousand things, one at a time. This book is also dedicated to Didier, whose death taught me there's nothing wrong with being a Normal Girl.

The most important thank yous are to My Family – Mom, Dad, Ken, Barbara and Grandpa Howie, Grandma and Pa Mann, and all my aunts, uncles, and cousins. I wouldn't be here without you.

This book could never have been written, could never have become a book, without the love and support of Mollie Doyle, editor, mentor, role model and sister. And I never would have written anything without the support and friendship of William Clark.

Thanks to my friends – Susan Cheever, Katy Roiphe, Fay and the whole Weldon clan, Judy Collins, Sue Shapiro, Aaron Hicklin, Susan Oaks, Nichole Beatie, Alice K., Cynthia F., Dr. Ross Brower, Patty Smalden, Annette Kulic, Lisa, Tara, Clare Patterson, Krissy Illey, Joan Collens and family, Sheri Fixel, Holly Solomon, Sally Painter, Lisa, and the crew at Holly Solomon Gallery, Edward Denoir, Naomi Wolf, Martian and Diana Weiss, and especially Jane, Josh, and George Radi Lines.

Thanks also to – Brian De Fiore, Lynn Goldberg, Brian Lipson, Rosie Boycott, Michelle Lavery, Glenda Bailey, A.G. Britton, Sue Fletcher, Katy, and everyone at Villard/Random House and Hodder. And, of course, Lowtar Minic.

And finally, thanks to Mike Weiss, who taught me about love, forgiveness, and wrestling.

∫

SCEPTRE

chapter one

I think it was Donna Rice or Donna Reed or maybe it was Diana Ross who said Andy Warhol's funeral was like a night at Studio 54. In that vein, Jeff's funeral is the equivalent of a night at Planet Hollywood. But it's all the same really: fast food, cocaine, and disco music. Nothing ever really changes, not around here anyway. Maybe disco has become techno, promiscuous sex has morphed into cautious promiscuous sex, and cell phones have replaced religion as the opiate of the masses, but our relentless obsession with The Next Best Thing-ism (TNBT-ism) remains the same.

If only it was as simple as me, the-out-of-it-never-really-It girl, trying to snort a bump in a speeding taxi. Brushing the cigarette ash off my black tunic, my eye catches a buttoned-down grandmother and her wiry granddaughter in her school kilt. Flying past them on Park Avenue, I have a brief moment of that there-is-something-really-wrong-with-your-life feeling. It passes before it can take me. The driver and I argue about which park crossing to take. Ignoring me, he turns abruptly, knocking my little pile of cocaine onto my suede boots. I run my fingers up and down on my shoes until I've wiped, sucked and licked every particle of cocaine from within the grains of suede. Then I lick my dusty fingers.

Call me an antisocial socialite, but this is my fifth funeral in July and I can't even keep my shoes clean. My grandmother, my aunt, three friends, and a distant cousin have died in the same ninety-one days making funeral attendance my new profession. I have worn black more in the last three months than I did in my entire Pablo Neruda reading phase. But all this goes with the territory, or so I assume, it's not exactly as if they tell you how to behave when you've murdered your boyfriend. And there's certainly no chapter in Emily Post's etiquette book on the how to's of attending your victim's funeral.

The temple grows out of the sidewalk on Fifth Avenue, a giant monument to rich Jews. The face of the building is slick, built with white bomb shelter brick strong enough to withstand the Nazis. There is nothing that could ever affect its structure, not the multitude of deaths mourned here, not the anorexia that wastes the female congregation, not Prozac that makes them comfortable, not even acid rain. I've been to lots of funerals at this temple; this is the first for someone I've murdered, though.

It's one of those hot, sticky, overcast days in July.

The kind of day, like every other July day in New York City, where your thighs stick to the plastic taxi seats. It's been an exhausting week – hang-overs, clumpy mascara, and working at the dreaded gallery. But it's over because it's Thursday and that's when my workweek ends. My plan is this: go to the funeral; make an appearance; mourn; spend no more than seven minutes alone with my mother; leave; go to Greenwich with some people I find at the funeral; when in Greenwich stay in mother's shrine to herself; raise my liver count; suppress my red blood cell count; deafen some nerve endings; and try to have a good time in the process. But I'm flex, except for the seven minutes part.

Funerals are the cotillions of the 'nineties, where the young people meet and mingle. All this might seem abnormal to you – like the fact that this congregation mourns the teenage sons of bankers, every day – but it's a little more compli-cated than that.

Filling the sidewalk with chatter from their cell phones, these glossy blow-dried mourners shine like they never had a problem in their perfectly choreographed lives. They aren't like us. The diffi-culties we normal people suffer slide right off their publicists' backs. Never having had an awkward phase, they live busy lives, adjusting their sun-glasses and making sure their unborn children have a place on the waiting list for the Dayton School. Some of them half-turn to look at me (maybe it's my dirty fingernails that make me not merit a full turn). I am the living embodiment of an awkward phase. But I must seem vaguely familiar to them, after all I've been mentioned on Page Six sixteen times, and I'm only nineteen.

I barely have room to move at this movie premiere masking as a funeral. There's a paparazzi line and everything, leaving me to wonder who they got to cater the Shiva. I really like chocolate rugulah. Of course I can't eat it, but I can smell it. My mother waits for me outside. She is covered in a highwaisted vintage Halston pantsuit that's a little too tight for someone of her advanced age somewhere in the ballpark of forty-five to sixty. Her almost invisible cellulite bubbles in a little bump around her waist. I love her small doll-like features and her soft voice. I love her little-ness. She is thin, in that willowy, dehydrated way all socialites are thin. Her short brown hair may have seen one too many hair dryers, but it still does the job of covering the scars behind her ears. She got her work done in Brazil, early 'eighties, hence the scars behind her ears. Good thing she didn't have the work done two countries over, then she'd probably have scars in the middle of her forehead. I lean down and kiss her forehead. Because both of us were calculating on the other's lateness, we have nearly missed each other.

'Are those my black burned velvet pants?' Holding the back of my shirt up, she inspects my butt for a confirmation that they are indeed her pants. 'Just making sure you've taken my favorite pants, the only pants that fit me, the ones with the green metallic lining and the feather attached to the back pocket.'

'No, hello. No, how are you doing at this tragic time?'

'Sorry, sweetie.' She takes my shoulders in a forced hug. I step back choking on her sickly-sweet perfume.

'Where did you get that perfume, It smells . . . hum . . . more dead cat than flower.' She frowns and I realize I've hurt her feelings. 'I'm sorry. It's nice, very nice and floral. Very floral.' I'm trying to behave like nothing is wrong, but the chatter in my head about Jeff, perfume, and the fact that I'd love another bump makes me feel otherwise. A family tree that reads like other people's resumés should guarantee some peace of mind. But I have this feeling where the peace of mind should be, and when I get this feeling . . .

'Miranda, go like this.' She points a rounded pink nail in my direction.

'What? Could you not stick your finger in my face?'

'You have something in your teeth.'

'Oh, where?' She points to the middle of the center of my teeth.

'Right there.' She sticks her fingernail into my teeth.

'Is it gone?' I look around to make sure that no one's looking at me, the tooth-picker. I have porcelain fronts on all my teeth, making it a challenge to extract things from in-between them.

'Here.' She sticks her finger in my teeth and pulls the piece of green foliage out. God knows how it got there. I haven't eaten solid food since the advent of Kate Moss, at least I think I haven't. 'There.' She smiles proudly. She's done with me, finished with her motherly moment. 'Let's go.'

We walk down the paparazzi line, like sad people at a funeral. Cameras flash but promptly stop when we pass in front of them – after all, an old socialite and her daughter: there's hardly a scandal in that. If they only knew.

'Should I smile?' I whisper. I just want to look normal. There is nothing wrong with me, no internal crisis that a Zanax couldn't reconcile.

'No, people don't smile at funerals. Keep your head down and look sad.'

Mom vogues for the cameras. She's someone who knows how to stick out her neck so her jowls, the jowls of an aging socialite, are stretched out, obscured by her damaged brown hair.

'Right, yeah, sad.' I'm not a shrink or anything, but I can say with some authority that it's been a long time since I've had a feeling that hasn't been a direct result of some drug I've taken. So the word sad just seems like another word that rolls down my tongue and out of my mouth.

'Come on, Miranda.' She sounds agitated, fidgety – she needs a nice stiff vodka tonic. 'I'd think you'd be good at this by now.'

'I'd think so too. But . . .'

'Yeah.'

'MMMMMirandaaaaaa.' I feel a shock run through my hair follicles from a voice that could make me bald. I turn, pulling my arm away from Mom's.

James Wool looks like a newspaper reporter but isn't. He talks like he's smart, which he also isn't. And he's natty like his tweed jacket. His lips are so far from my cheek when he air kisses me, he's still in the 718 area code.

'Well, well. How is everybody's little vixen?'

'Hi, James.'

'Wasn't he young? Isn't this sad? Horrible really? Didn't you see this coming? I didn't, but you must have. Didn't you? Can you believe he was so young?' James doesn't engage in normal conversation, instead he shoots questions in the general direction of the person he's talking at. Doesn't he know I was trained as a charming dinner companion, not as an intellectual?

'No, Yes, Yes, Yes . . . Yes, No, well twenty-nine isn't that young, but it's young to die. I guess.' Personally, I can't imagine why anyone would want to live past twenty-one, after all, doctors recommend standard colonoscopies every year after turning fifty, blah. All that gastroenterology aside, most people don't die three months after turning twenty-nine. I almost reach for his hand, but then I remember we Wokes don't do that kind of thing.

People push past us. James doesn't move. I need him to go away.

'So, Miranda. Tell me what are we up to these days?' James lived in England for one semester in college. Ever since then he's had a voice plagued with annoying euro-isms.

'Nothing. I'm working at the gallery two days a week now, which is really interfering with my martini schedule, and I'm supposed to be involved in this project with paintings. Some group-show for women. But I just can't get inspired. So I've decided to go to parties until the inspiration hits me.'

'Brilliant brilliant.' Even his chuckle is patronizing as he plays with his glasses, as if to say he finds inanimate objects more interesting than me. 'I mean, how many times does one get to be nineteen?'

'Right. But James, most people here think I'm twenty-two so don't tell them I'm nineteen.' He looks at me as if to say, this is exactly what he expects from someone like me. 'Do you swear?'

'I wonder why everyone doesn't just drop out of college and paint. I wonder why everyone doesn't do exactly what they want to.'

'Gee. I don't know. They should. Come out of the closet much?'

'I must find my wife. Ciao. Ciao.' He walks away, thank God. I watch his feet until I can no longer differentiate his baby blue Hush Puppies from anyone else's.

People file in – socialites, models, and various up-towners. This is either a funeral or a fashion show, because there aren't enough seats. I slide onto the wooden bench wedging myself between Mom and the armrest that ends the bench. Mom sits next to Jeff's leathery mother, who clocks enough hours at Capri Tanning Center to be considered more handbag than woman.

I am surrounded. Behind me is the Southampton, Upper East Side crowd, on my right is the rich and old, Upper West Side communist-turned-capitalist contingent. To my left is the 'I want to be an editor, so buy me a magazine' group. Eurotrash is in the back left corner and defrocked royalty in the back right corner. The group has sorted and divided itself in minutes.

'Miranda.' Someone's hand is on my shoulder, invading that invisible barrier of what is mine versus what is yours. I flinch; there are two people who can touch me. One of them is dead and the other is not Whit. I know it's Whit because I can hear the drag of his umbrella on the tile and I can smell him – even from thirty feet away the subtle mixture of Halston cologne, cigars, and vodka permeates the membrane. Since I've known him, he's always carried an umbrella. It's possible that even if it were never to rain again, he'd still carry an umbrella. I brush his hand off my shoulder as if it were dandruff.

'Whit, what are you doing here?' I whisper. 'You didn't even know him.'

'We can't all be friends with the A-list. But it's a free country, I can surely attend anyone's funeral.' Whit and I met through Crown Princess Marie of Belize (before she died of a mysterious form of pneumonia, a.k.a. AIDS). He felt familiar to me, something Harvard in the way he lectured me, something impressive in his vast knowledge of all those books longer than a thousand pages that I hadn't even started. I had a rare moment of good judgement and didn't let him seduce me. I think that won his respect.

'Whit, you look so handsome,' I say flirting, lying.

'You think? How's life in the art world treating you?'

'Use the word life lightly.'

'Well how is it?' he says, fishing for a problem to solve.

'You, know the usual. Answering the phone, staring into space, checking my voice mail, keeping one eye out for the future Mr Woke.' I look around trying to find someone cute to make eye contact with to rescue me from this conversation. 'So, tell me about how busy you are.'

'What do you mean?' He's so obnoxious.

'I'm sure you're very busy, right?' Something busy that will never materialize into a paycheck or even a mention.

'Hiiiiiiiii, Whit you look so handsome.' Clearly Mom and I have reviewed the same social manual: *The Woke Way for Wakes, Shiva, and Funerals.*

'Hello, Diana.' Whit hates my mother, for a number of reasons. Reason number one: he is appalled by her 50' x 50' closet filled with enough Manolo Blahnik shoes to bring a third world Country out of famine.

She puts her arm around my shoulder and I shake her off.

'Mom.' She senses my annoyance. Maybe I could get high from smoking my boots, there's probably enough cocaine in between the grains of suede, but I can't imagine smoking suede is that much fun.

'Well . . .' Her cell phone rings and with this she descends into the level of hell reserved only for dermatologists who advertise on subways and socialites who talk on cell phones at funerals. 'I'm sorry, darling.'

'What are you sorry for?' I talk down to her.

A few manicured nails dismiss me with the 'I'm talking on my cell phone at a funeral' sign. And yet another mortifying mommy moment has taken place.

'What is she saying?' Whit leans a little too close to me. I shake my head as if to say I don't know.

Lucy Sunningdale winks at Mom as if to say 'Hey comrade of the mutual admiration society.' (That should make Mom happy, if she notices.) Whit is dressed in layers, blue shirt under gray vest, under brown jacket, under plaid scarf, all under a bowler hat. I wonder how long it takes him to pile on all that clothing in the morning.

'So Whit, what are you working on these days?'

'I'm working on a project with Mary Westheimer. You must know who she is?'

I do. 'No.'

'Miranda.' He looks at me like I've never had a thought in my life. 'She's *the* pinnacle, *the most* famous, *most* important female artist in the world and *I* am dong her next piece.'

'But you're not an artist.'

'Miranda you need to listen, that's your problem. I didn't say that, I said I was doing her next piece. You're cripplingly literal. That's your problem – black and white, literal thinking. You kill me.'

I hope not. I can only handle being responsible for one person's death.

He looks at my shaking hand. I try to hold my left hand still with my right. 'What?'

He looks at me, with that I-know-what-your-problem-is-because-I-took-psychology-in-college look.

'What?'

'You have been seeming the tiniest bit odd lately; I mean not that odd but a little . . . a little bit off.'

I try to move away from him. 'Is it hot in here or what?'

He moves his face closer to mine. 'Really. I just think you might, I don't know, be taking too many sleeping pills. That might be your problem.'

'Ah. No.'

'You seem. I don't know . . . ' Seem like a murderer? I'd go with that, after all I think I just killed my boyfriend. He inhales really hard and looks at me.'. . . thinner.'

'New diet.' I smile.

'Yeah.'

'I've lost fifteen pounds, I needed to lose the weight. You remember how blubberous I was when I came back from London.'

'Yeah. You were huge. Massive. Now that was bloat, my God that was bloat.' He plays with the handle of his umbrella.

'Thanks.'

'But, I know the diet you're on.' He smiles.

'What? You mean the 'eighties diet: all cocaine and grapefruit, all the time.'

'Not funny.'

'Whit, save the value judgements. New topic. I really don't think any of this is your business anyway.'

He nods. 'If you don't want it to be my business then don't wear a tank top. What the hell happened to you? You look like you've been in some kind of bar brawl.' He points at the bruises that run the length of my arms, a casual reminder of my last night with Jeff.

'Whatever. Maybe . . . ' I look around. This conversation is droning on, so I interject an anyway, the universal sigh for let's end this conversation. 'Anyway,' I sigh.

And right on cue, 'Oh, there's my dear friend Alex.' A mass of golden brown curly hair walks by us. Whit waves furiously. Those tresses can claim responsibility for seducing every woman under thirty-five in the art world.

'Whit.'

'What?' He says as he turns toward Alex and his hair.

'I don't know how you can say Alex is your closest friend. I was at a party with him and when I dropped your name, there was no recognition. No flicker that he ever knew what I was talking about, it was like I was speaking Portuguese,' I whisper.

'Your problem is you need to see a doctor. Get help.' Whit leaves me to go chase after Alex.

I turn back to Mom, who has somehow started talking to Slone Billbinder. It's lifeboats on the Titanic, cocktail party syndrome. 'So, Slone what's the new hair color for fall?' Mom asks as if she's discussing Kierkegaard.

'White-gray on the under-twenty set . . . and black on the over-thirty group. I just love the new fall cut, too. It's soo cute. It's going to look beyond super perfect on Miranda. Marcus, you know Marcus my husband? Anyway, he thinks Miranda would look great in a sort of modified Paula Jones look. I like to think of the cut as a PJ – modern yet functional yet political.' Slone never fidgets. Her hands are attached to skinny arms which are attached to tiny shoulders. Her other bones stick out at fashionable right-angles. Her white-blond hair sits in a loose knot and is wispy the way soap opera stars are when engaged in conversation. She is the kind of woman who stuffs her dead cats and displays them lovingly on the coffee table. I don't even have a coffee table.

'Yeah?' I look at both of them. Is this normal funeral conversation?

'Miranda. You look so cute darling. Really thin.' Slone squeezes my shoulder to articulate her point. I'm gonna bet Ms Billbinder never murdered any of *her* boyfriends or ex-husbands.

'Well. If it seems like it'll look good on her, then I want her to have that hair cut. I think she needs a new look. In fact, I'm buying her a whole new fall wardrobe. She's been somewhat depressed. I think this will perk her up. Don't you, Slone?'

'Mom. God. Don't waste your time I'll just have Dr Berkenstein up my Prozac.'

'Excuse me.' Mom takes a tone that sounds suspiciously like an authority figure. Billbinder seems a little taken aback.

'What? It's the nineties, I can't talk about psychopharmacology at a funeral? At least give me that.'

Janice taps me hard on the shoulder. 'Hey, kiddo,' she quietly mouths. I am kiddo because for all practical purposes I am all of ten years old in the mind of fashion aficionado, former model, former and current junkie, former wife of, and former stripper Janice.

'Hey, Janice, we were just talking about Prozac. Want to join in? What are your thoughts on the subject of psychopharmacology?' She smiles at me as if to say shut up. She hugs me and I can feel her ribs though her sheer silk designer blouse. She turns her back to us to go rub ribs with some girl who looks like a refugee but is actually the bearer of the new calf for Calvin clam diggers. She leaves and the smell of Chanel No. 5 lingers, almost blocking out the formaldehyde smell of funeral, which is a taste thousands of grams of cocaine can't cover.

The noise starts to subside. The rabbi enters. For a moment there is silence, just breath. Maybe for a half second I have the feeling everything might be OK, the pressure falls from my shoulders and the silence makes my ears ring. Then the rabbi starts to speak and so does everybody else.

The rabbi introduces Jeff's plastic-y sister and hobbles off the stage. Jeff's sister waxes Upper East Side Melrose Place. She had a Porsche in high school and used it, or more accurately the back seat of it, to give all the popular boys blow jobs while Billy Joel whined out 'Piano Man'. At the time, her tendency towards Billy Joel seemed more offensive than her slutty-ness. She gets up and starts to lose herself in her sentences. In a disconcerting muddle she looks at me harshly like I murdered her brother, which I did.

Jeff only wore black and grey. He's wearing a black suit even now in his half-open casket. Some brilliant make-up artist has hidden his dead-ness from all of us. In fact he has never looked better than he does right now. He's certainly never smelled better than he does right now – he used to always smell of burnt Tums (a.k.a. crack), sex, and cigarettes.

Jeff and I never quite worked as lovers. It seemed the harder I tried, the meaner he got. I should have pulled up stakes a long time ago. But as with everything else in my life there came a point where I didn't have a choice anymore, a time when, like the drugs, he was as much me as I was.

What little of Jeff's sister's body is naturally hers is draped in a grey suit and ice blue shirt. I sweat a lot; I'd sweat right through that kind of soft chambray. Her smart blond Wasp hair and blue eyes promise her at the very least marriage to a money guy and the fifteen rooms on Fifth Avenue that follow suit. Nobody is quiet. Whit smiles at some model four seats over. I wonder if she's married.

I turn back and look at Janice. She's flirting with the new and soon to be ex editor of *Mavda* magazine, *Mavda* magazine vibing with hipness, oozing from every well-formatted-contrived-embellished story about the men who live dangerously in high-end retail stores around Manhattan. Typical, she can't quite pick the winners. Behind me, the row is filled with journalists like David Faxem, a notorious *Speak* magazine hit man defined by his love of hotel rooms that rent by the hour and my personal brainchild, the seventeen-martini lunch. David earns his frequent flyer miles with trips to Hazelden. He rubs leather-padded shoulders with Janice's gay husband James Wool. James Wool is an artistic genius or so says Upper East Side Jewish *Socialite* magazine, which is always wrong about everything, but maybe he's a genius babysitter, having cut his teeth on the Schnabel kid.

'Are those pants last season's?' David whispers at me.

'Fuck off.'

'I thought I saw them on the rack at Lohman's.' I turn around and smile at David, who smiles at James. Mom, who has radar for anything about herself, tunes in and whispers, 'Those pants look fab on you, don't listen to them.'

Brett gazes across the room and settles in at the podium. The law of cocaine physics dictates that he'll never make eye contact with a single congregation member, the tear of sweat on his forehead further assures this. He struggles with the microphone as if he has something urgent to say. I can see his face try to muster the right brand of emotion.

'He's Mafia,' I whisper in Mom's ear.

'Prove it.'

'Isn't the suit proof enough?'

'I won't buy that theory until I see a body in the trunk, Miranda.'

Brett is a Five Towns Jew. Everything from his patent leather shoes to his baggy blue suits that were hand picked by his mother at Today's Man, tell us this. His accent is unchanged from the Holy Land (Long Island), and his nose lacks the surgical de-enhancement that we Upper East Side Jews know so well. Brett is the antithesis of Diet Judaism. My family is a case study in Diet Jews. Diet-Jews are different, we rarely belong to a temple, we use the Maxwell House Hagaddah and shun all of the Five Towns (each town a little more than the one before). We celebrate one High Holiday. (We just celebrate it five times a year. 'Which holiday is the egg and lamb holiday and which holiday is the one with the cookies that look like hats?')

Brett has good Hugh Grant hair, but he's fat. He thinks he's a sculptor. but his mother is still waiting for him to become a podiatrist. He'd sue me for thinking this.

It's immaterial what he said or how he said it. Brett gave us everything he had. Unfortunately, he didn't have much.

The next person to torture us is yet another rabbi, then a cantor, and then Jeff's small tan mother gives us a speech that covers each of her past lives in painful detail – a blatant over-share. I'd give her performance a nine out of ten, she's almost at the Shirley McLaine level.

'You still awake, kiddo.' Janice, her pearls, and her cigarette breath lean over me. Ten years in New York and she still can't quite free herself from that southern twang of an accent.

'Somewhat awake. Somewhat asleep.'

'Shall we go powder our noses?'

'Fab. Mom, tell me what I miss.'

'I'll take notes.'

I hate it when anyone touches me, but none of my rules mean anything with Janice. When we talk incessantly about nothing, she puts her hand in mine and I hold on. She applies a layer of false eyelashes in the mirror and then leaves me alone with the sink and some lines of coke spread out on the wash board. Snorting coke makes the voices stop. Each line burns with the promise of an escape that I'm still waiting for.

The stall door slams shut and I can hear the lighter under the spoon, the popping boiling that heroin makes, like Jiffy Pop with kick. I never shoot up. OK, OK, OK. Rarely, do I shoot up. She tightens the belt. While I can't see her because she has done me the service of closing the door, I certainly can hear her squirm under the pressure of her cashmere belt, now conveniently working as an alternative to a tourniquet. The tapping of three polished fingers grows louder and louder, until she finds a vein. I can hear her groan as the needle pierces her skin and I hear her arm hit the side of the stall, as it goes limp with the gentle floating feeling. I hope she gets rid of the bloody syringe. I hate looking at other people's used kits.

She comes out of the stall looking horrible, more awful than usual. 'God, Janice go easy.' Wetting a paper towel and kicking my foot under the bathroom door, I try to wipe the blood off her arm and the drool from her chin. She looks at me with void eyes, a junkie who doesn't know any better. I sit her on the floor and watch her come back from that place that isn't quite death, but isn't quite life either. I smile at her knowing she isn't looking. I like secretly watching the life come back into her features, white lips go pink, cheeks rose up, then her eyes recognize me again. Her hands shake and it's clear to both of us she's just trying to get straight, chasing a high lost years ago. Somehow I find all of this comforting, always thinking the death of one of us would be the end of all of us, but clearly my suspicions were wrong, further proof that nothing ever changes around here. When she looks better, I stand her up so that she can lean on to the sink to put on some lipstick.

'Are you OK?'

'Yeah.'

'Good.' I look into the mirror at both of us. She shakes, turning on the tap. The water makes a noise like rivers in the country, far away from the dirt of the city.

'Are you sure?' I look back at her. She doesn't look OK, but what heroin addict does?

'God, Miranda, would you please stop being so hysterical.'

'Never.' We smile at each other.

'Good.'

'That husband of yours is quite a gem.'

'Why? What did James do? He is such a bad boy. Never can quite keep him on his leash.'

'Just the usual.' Her eyes are dark again, a sure sign that yet another trip to Bellevue is on the horizon. The skin on Janice's face has started to recede back into the bone, as if I'm losing her to herself. Her hands are dry and red with eczema, a contrast to her skin, which is an unearthly white the color of fake teeth. All the rehabs, all the fresh starts, all the midnight ambulance trips to Lenox Hill, Mt Sinai, and Harlem's splendid North General Hospital.

'Miranda, what about James?'

'Oh, forget it. I don't want to miss the end. I love my religion. I'm sure the rabbi is saying something fabulously enlightening right now and we're missing it.'

She smiles, 'You always had a thing for him.'

'Though I do like nebbishy. But the rabbi seems a little old for me.'

Our eyes meet with half smiles and for a moment I feel something. I feel like we're sisters. She smoothes the creases of my tunic, and touches my hair and I let her.

Mom's whispering into her cell phone when I squeeze back into my place on the bench.

'Mom.'

'What?'

'It's a funeral.' She clicks down on her cell phone.

'I love you.' She runs her fingers though my hair.

'Don't touch me.'

'Fine.'

'Stop, I want to listen.'

Fine. Miranda.'

'Sushhhhhhh.'

chapter two

I leave the temple feeling empty, the entire texture of the morning felt more like Oreo filler than anything remotely satisfying. I guess the only thing to do is chalk it all up to another morning lost.

I make a decision to try to be as productive with my afternoon as possible. After all I did get out of bed, though why is still a mystery to me. I've been trying to up my productivity by productively looking for someone with drugs, but I'm having trouble seeing anything with these sunglasses, blinding in their chic-ness. Maybe I'm taking too much Prozac, but the clear afternoon light makes everything look beautiful. Not to harp on the Prozac thing, but the wonder drug seems to have cut some of the anxiety I have about murdering my boyfriend. I'm glad I double-dosed with my morning Pepsi One. I look at my small paisley Halstoned mother, and deep inside my brain rushing with coke-induced seratonin I know that taking a life can never be fixed. Not even by her.

But who wants to come back anyway? I've had my breakfast cereal and domesticity and it wasn't that great.

I glance at a cluster that forms what I call the Madison Avenue Mafia. Anyone who says the Madison Avenue Mafia (MAM, my second mother of a sort) doesn't have principles is guilty of an egregious over-simplification. MAM operates under the basic principles of Zen Buddhism: mindfulness. They might not be mindful of you or me, but they make up for it with a self-obsession so blinding that the sun looks tame. There is just one principle: no matter how large the nose or how bad the birthmark, whatever it is it'll look better waxed, tweezed, trained, starved and squeezed into a mini skirt. Eventually you'll have a product, one that has been honed, perfected. One that will be married before the end of the summer season. Buy her a Jitney ticket and send her out to Southampton.

Cousin Sidney stands among the MAM, a footnote in other sick people's lives, with her gawky goyische blondness that has methodically seduced every single gossip page in this city. Cousin Sidney earned her red nose the way any good alcoholic does: with screaming matches at cocktail parties and a notorious appetite for tennis pros and ski instructors. But now Sid's notoriety has worn thin, her face-lift fell a long time ago and she just hangs on by her silk tips.

Sad Sidney Woke with her dead son, David,

stolen from his mother when he was only thirteen. She may never live the headline down. He
was just riding someone else's motorcycle,
smoking someone else's dope with someone else's
friends, fulfilling someone else's destiny and then
in a flash and a tree stump he was gone as if he
were never there. Most people don't understand
what it's like to think you were born to die. It's
like a virus that grows and infects everything until
you're just another self-fulfilling prophecy,
another 'I saw it coming.'

I am of the school of thought that other people's
dead children are all essentially the same, eco-
nomic messes: they leave no wife, no myriad of
old books, no rent-controlled apartment. I
respected David for not having friends. Loneliness
and isolation were David's most charming character traits. Sid doesn't look at me, and I almost stop
her to tell her I miss David. But I don't miss him
at all. In fact, I've really forgotten he was ever
alive.

Low boughs of trees form a canopy over our
heads and the sun indirectly touches us as we
pour onto the street. I have an intense allergic
reaction to the flowers that surround me and
sneeze all over Jeff's family's PR girl to my left.
She winces and slithers off to find something
quotable, making a charming face that reflects
years of her Polish ancestors sleeping with their
sisters.

Mom is playing with a half-lit cigarette. She

doesn't know how to smoke, but she thinks she does. So it's smoke-cough-smoke-cough-cough-smoke, and she stomps the cigarette out on the pavement – think Olivia Newton John in the final scene of *Grease*. Mom's browsing for husband number six. I suspect it's just a matter of time until another new dad comes into the picture.

'Do you want to share a taxi across the park?' Janice waves her arm in the air and her brown bangle slides down it.

'I'm going home. Someone's got to do some work in this family.' But what does Mom do? She supposedly 'manages the house', which mostly consists of screaming at her staff and going to 'appointments' – afternoons at the Plaza Athenée with a certain tan society journalist or visits to various shrinks sprinkled all over the Upper West and Upper East Sides. 'And Miranda, would you pleeease let go of my arm. I mean really.' She glares at me. I realize I've been holding on for dear life. All this makes me think Janice is a miracle of modern science, an ambulatory heroin addict, a marvel.

'Janice, I don't think I'm going to Shiva,' I say, half looking at her perfectly rounded red toes, each the mirror of the one before it. My toes are not perfectly rounded and on a good day they are chipped red. I wonder if the woman who did her feet saw the tracks on her calves when she lifted her skirt. She pulls together the buttons on her red jacket. She looks like the Mad Hatter, but taller and madder.

'Why not? Mick's going to be there.'

'Who?'

'Mick as in Jagger as in the Rolling Stones.'

'When did he become Mick to you? There's an assumption of familiarity, that isn't yours to make!'

'How do you know?'

'I don't, but anyway I highly doubt that Mick Jagger is going to be at Jeff's Shiva. Even if he is, I don't necessarily want to go. What's so great about Mick Jagger anyway?'

'Well.' She stops to think. I'm really over her thinking.

'He's older than my mother.'

'Yeah, and?'

'Um, I don't know?' An innocent smile, a hunch, a little hair in my mouth.

'Why don't you want to go? "I don't know" doesn't seem to explain a whole lot, Randa. I think you can do better than that with me.'

I scrunch my eyes up all tight. 'Because I miss Jeff and this will make me think of him.' Or because I think I killed him by preparing a needle with an air bubble in a sleazy hotel room somewhere in Atlantic City, and it kills me that I can't even remember what happened.

She looks at me for a moment too long. I think she understands why I don't want to go, why I can't go.

'It's OK.' Janice almost touches my hand, but glides off before I can think to touch her back.

'Janice!' The sun feels hot. Some coke would be nice.

'Yeah?' She looks at me but keeps walking. She was one of the first models to get collagen injected into her already prominent cheekbones. And when the collagen fell, started floating around her face, the modeling agency suggested she might take a little vacation from the lens. She hasn't been back since.

'Janice.' Janice has coke.

'Miranda. What?' It feels like everyone is looking at me and they might be. I have that crazed 'I need a hit' look in my eyes.

'Janice, I need to talk to you.'

'We just did.' She looks at me, and then at the vacant socialite she's standing next to. 'We are among friends here.' I feel myself coming down and at this point I would sell my mother for another hit. I would most likely sell my mother anyway, but . . .

'I need a hit.'

'What?' She smiles, sharing in the pride that being a drug addict trumps being a socialite any day. I know exactly what she wants, she wants me to say it louder.

'I need a hit.' The socialite's clear blue eyes expand in horror.

Jeff's family starts sliding into big black shiny cars, and I wonder if any of them are going to have to suffer though the stifling July heat – all of them air-conditioned nightmares in their own right.

Janice moves closer.

I hold her shoulders, like I am older than she is. She has bones for shoulders, fleshless. 'I think we should go to Greenwich for the weekend.'

'What about your mother?'

'She's staying in the city to take ice fishing lessons.'

'Really?'

'Well, I was thinking, which I try never to do, as a card-carrying member of the nothing-to-say-generation. But I can always make room in the brain for a little advanced blow planning . . . call it blow brain.' She nods. 'Me, you, and some very fine strychnine makes three.' As I say strychnine, I see Brett out of the corner of my eye.

None of my ex-boyfriends wants to have any-thing to do with me except for Brett, who doesn't get the ex part. The ex part of ex is lost on him, even though it's been three long months, filled with me sleeping with his friends. He slides around me, and smiles: he wants to talk. We haven't spoken since the night that Jeff died and I came to with him pulling me off Jeff's body as I kicked and screamed. Brett's waiting for me, but I'm not waiting for him.

'Yeah, strychnine.'

'All we need is some black clothing and some clean needles. And we'll be in Greenwich in an hour.' Brett's lurking a few feet away, turning back every few seconds to see if Janice and I are done talking.

There is a long pause while Janice considers her options. It takes a while for her neurons to jump the cerebral wall and the synapses to meet in thought. 'Gas up the black car, let's hit the road, Thelma.'

'Game on.' I say slapping her palm.

'Goodbyes.' She smiles almost gleefully. The goodbye portion of any social event is the most important. Janice will now pass out business cards and air kiss until her air lips are chapped and her supply of business cards is gone – she won't even have one left to help her find her way home. I light a cigarette. Slowly dragging in, I try not to look around in the hope of avoiding the inevitable Brett ambush. But before I can even have a thought he's on me, all smiles and salutations. Did I mention I hate funerals?

'Miranda, you look great. How are you doing?'

'I'm fine. How are you, Brett?'

'Good. I was thinking about you.'

'Well don't strain that brain of yours. You're gonna need it some day. Though for what I have no idea.'

'Nice.'

'I saw your show at Dean's gallery. Great show. Genius. How'd you get the frosting on the giant mattress? And then to display it in a coffin? The ingenuity.' I look over his shoulder at the taxis that spin down Fifth Avenue.

He bows his head as if he's the only sculptor (mattress-frosting-artist?) in all of Manhattan who's uncomfortable being called a genius. 'Really?' Maybe he'd be less embarrassed if he knew I was lying.

'Yeah, great show.'

'So.' There are new taxis now, ones that look like mini-vans. When did this happen? How did I miss this?

'So.'

'How's your life? You seeing anybody?' This is the kind of question single ex-boyfriends should not ask.

'Bad. No.'

'You still with that old married guy?'

'No.'

'The Arab?' Brett looks at the ground.

'Nope, No more Ramadan for me. Anyyywayyy. I'm really glad we had this filler, it felt like it was almost a conversation. But now I've 1 got to—'

'Miranda, did I hear that you're going to Greenwich this weekend?'

'Yeah. Are you doing art openings this weekend?'

'Maybe.'

'If you go to openings, invite Jeff. I don't think Jeff's getting out enough.'

'No, he's probably not getting out enough. Miranda?'

'What?' I say with mild annoyance.

'That casket is confining but . . .'

'What?' Reality has always been my problem. 'Oh, my God. I spaced.' I need some coke, no, not some, a lot. I need a lot of coke. Doesn't have to be good coke, anything would be fine. But I need it now, now, now.

'Miranda.'

'What?'

'I think you have the wrong idea.'

'ME? I have no ideas about anything. You know that.'

'I'm trying to make you feel better.'

'I know you are. But don't. It's a waste of time, there's really only one thing that makes me feel better.'

'Stop being so fucking smart. You're so God damned precious. I don't know what's gonna kill you first, that brain of yours or the blow.'

'I really don't need another lecture.' The crowd of people is slowly thinning out to a few stragglers on the sidewalk. The party's over. Steve Rebell's been dead for years, and it's time to go back to the loneliness of our respective homes.

'But Randa. There's something I need to tell you.'

'Why don't you save it for someone who's listening?'

The West Side Highway snakes out of New York City. As we scream along the curves of the road, we narrowly escape a meaningful conversation and an unfortunate end with a school bus.

Janice and I sing along to a top forty station, Z100, everyone's favorite conflicted mix of rap and easy listening. Janice has perfect pitch and I'm tone deaf. Unfortunately I'm not a smooth enough driver for her to be able to fix in the car, so she sings.

'What are you thinking about?' She has a brown and gold Hermes scarf over her loose brown hair. She's the kind of woman who gets dressed up to look casual.

'I don't know.' I scream over the voice on the radio. 'Can I have one more bump of strychnine (cocaine)? I'll close the roof.'

'But, Ms Miranda, you're driving.'

I pick both hands up off the steering wheel. 'I hardly consider this driving, it's more like sitting behind the steering wheel.'

'Sweetheart, you're out of control.'

'You think?'

Two and a half grams of cocaine later, we arrive in Greenwich. Mom shipped the driveway gravel in from Italy, courtesy of husband number four's lucrative foray in strip-mining. If only husband number four had outlived the driveway, but ah that is the socialite rub.

Each room of the house is a carefully contrived experiment in self-indulgence, representing a life created for that very thing. Each of the ten bedrooms has its own obnoxious theme. The Venice Room is decorated with yellow blown glass horses. The Coastal Room is filled with conch shells, sand, and stuffed sturgeons. The Western Room is so authentic it smells like horseshit.

I sit on a long wicker armchair and pretend to soak in the severe nature of rural Greenwich. Janice has disappeared into some bathroom so she can dose herself yet again with heroin. The uncomfortable wicker chair makes indents in my legs and all the other places where the flesh used to be.

It seems like a long time passes before Janice appears again. This time she's really lit, her long feet almost touch the grass path that leads to the pool. She comes and sits down beside me, forcing me to turn and look directly into the sun so that I have to squint to see her.

I'll admit it's hard to know if someone like Janice likes you or merely finds you a convenience. It may be it's her dubious smile or the sound of her giggle or the way she snickers after every word. There is something hooker-like about her, maybe it is the state of all aging Glit Girls: unable to fade, they rot, and all of their former Glitness, glibness, wastes away, falls off the bone. She lights a joint and it smells like decaying orange peel.

'I don't know what the hell's wrong with you, Miranda.' Janice says, passing me the joint. 'Is it something with Brett? Did he say something to make you this way?'

'No. He didn't do anything.'

'Well then what the hell is it?' Heroin addicts are not social workers. I might do better looking for compassion somewhere else.

'Janice. Don't you think it's a big deal? Jeff is dead.'

'That's why we went to his funeral.'

'Janice, we just went to a funeral. Jeff's funeral. The man is DEAD. Do you understand what that means? He's not going to be at the Whitney junior party next week. He's not going to be at the Whitney ever again.'

'And that's a bad thing?'

'The dead part's gotta suck. Don't you think?' I gingerly take a hit off the joint she passes me to 'calm my Jewish nerves'.

'Darling there is nothing to be hysterical about. What to do with my little drama queen?' She pats me on the head, turns, and pulls her dress over her head. Skin and bones, she jumps into the pool. It's amazing, even in her most deranged drugged-out state she's still very OK-looking.

'There's nothing to do with me,' I shout at the pool as she glides under water. I hold the joint up to my lips and then decide I'm not going to smoke pot anymore. I've made this decision about 30,000 times, but this time I'm sure. It feeds my coke paranoia and it's bad for my lungs and it feels like crap. To punctuate this momentous decision, I grind the joint into my mother's Italian gravel. But I've already sucked back most of the thing.

It occurs to me that Janice is either stupid or impenetrably narcissistic. She chalks my anxiety up to Judaism, and all my other problems up to anxiety. 'You have to relax.' She appears from under the water, smiles, and puts out her hand for a cigarette. I place the long white cigarette in her fingers. There is something creepy about her knobby fingers, which jut out in red bumps where the knuckles are.

'Relax? How?' I say.

'I don't know. There must be some Deepak (Chopra) tapes lying around somewhere.'

She swims over to me an awkward mess, all bones and neurosis.

'Did you find the Deepak?'

'No. I forgot to look.'

'What's wrong with you?'

'I hate my life.'

'Why don't we have a party?' This is Janice's stock answer for any problem. That's not to say I disagree with her thinking.

'Sure.'

'You're alright? Aren't you sweetie?' When I lift my eyelids, it's fair to assume I may have mixed too much alcohol with my Valium. Dosage has never been my forte. I can see the sky and it's blatantly dark. This is alarming, because if there is anything heroin chic has taught me it's that if you can see the sky then you must be lying on your back. 'See, I told you she was fine. See Whit, she's just fine.'

'Janice.' Janice kneels on the floor, staring at me. I try to sit up. Brett leans over and puts his hand on my forehead. He looks over me like the doctor he should be.

'She doesn't look well.' Brett says.

'What? Get off me. I'm fine. God. If it's not people lecturing me, it's people touching me. Would everyone get their hands off me. Brett what are you doing here?'

'Miranda. You're fine, right? Nod if you're fine. See everyone, she's fine.' There are ten people I've never seen in my life hovering around me.

'Don't worry about me, I'll be just fine.'

'Come on, Miranda. I'll take you to the bathroom to clean up.' Ha, famous last words. Brett pulls me to my feet. Janice disappears into the house.

Brett smiles at me and drags me to a tiny yellow downstairs bathroom. It has lots of mirrors and very little light. As we all know, the less light, the fewer wrinkles.

Brett is fumbling with vials, caps, sunglasses, and pocket mirrors. Who wears sunglasses at night? My ex-boyfriend. He adjusts his sunglasses and lays out the mirror, the razor, and the hundred-dollar bill.

'Here.'

'Thanks.'

'You're welcome, sweetheart.' He puts his hand on my back.

I snort. He empties yet another small glass vial on the counter. 'So, how was the food?' I take his hand off my back.

'Where?'

'At the wedding, where do you think?' I snort a lot of cocaine and then more. I don't know when it is that I realize I'm gonna have to finish the whole thing, forgetting if I want to or not.

'Fine. They had chocolate rugalah.' He doesn't look at me.

'I didn't go.'

'I noticed.' He lays out another bunch of lines. I press down on the left nostril. Snort with the right.

'I bet his sister wasn't too happy.'

'What do you think, Randa?' He still isn't looking at me.

'I think she's not the sharpest knife in the drawer.'

'I hate to think of what you say about me when I'm not around.' Brett parcels out what he has left.

'Then don't think about it. Why are you thinking anyway? Besides, I'm hardly saying anything you don't already know about her. Face it, she's not the sharpest tack in the box, not the liveliest fish in the stream, not the smartest guest on Jerry Springer.'

'Randa, what's wrong with you?'

'Nothing. I mean I'm a crazy cocaine addict with a hankering for heroin. but other than that, I'm just a nice Jewish girl from the Upper East Side with Prada shoes. How could anything be wrong?'

'That's not what I'm talking about.'

'Well share, enlighten me.'

'Where's your sympathy? Her brother just died.'

'Listen to me, Brett,' I say, climbing up to the top of my soapbox. 'Nobody knows Jeff is dead as well as I do.'

'I know you think you had something to do with his . . . ' He stops. 'You didn't do anything wrong. I wish you could see that. I have this idear . . .'

'You have an idear, an idear. Why don't you just have an idea like the rest of us.'

'Shut the fuck up. God you're a fucking horror sometimes. A bitter nineteen-year-old. What did the world do to you that was so bad?'

'It made me ugly.'

'Are you kidding?'

'No.'

'What are you talking about? You're perfect: perfect white skin like ivory, perfect green eyes, perfect white teeth. Perfect red hair, slightly wavy. Beautiful, you're like some kind of princess. Some kind of doomed princess.'

'You just don't get it.'

'What?'

'I'm a waste of my parents' valuable resources. Don't you get it? All of this is about return. Make an investment, expect a return. It's simple. My shares are plummeting.'

'What are you talking about?'

'What am I not talking about?'

'I'm so sorry for you. You know that.'

'What the fuck is there to be sorry for?'

'You.'

'Shut up. Brett. You don't get it. Story of your fucking life you not getting it.'

I'm crying now, though I don't know why. 'I love you.' The coke isn't working, I'm not getting high.

'I need to get out of this bathroom. It feels very small in here.' And I'm right, there is something very small about the two of us alone in a bathroom where the ugly yellow wallpaper stares down at us like we did something to upset it.

The living room looks like it could have been an adverse reaction to Y2K it's so stuffed with floral chintz and other grand nineteenth century fabrics. All the lamps are made of hand-blown glass and all the tables are Louis XIV, gold and red. I need to get home, to find a way home, to find a home.

Janice has clearly picked up the hostessing duties in my absence, and while she's no Martha Stewart, she has managed to find the only gossip columnist in the room. David Stall is finished routing through my mother's underwear drawer and is now laughing at Janice's knock-knock jokes.

I notice an army of my junkie friends breaking Wedgwood plates à la Greek wedding.

Someone hands me a large Stoli tonic with no ice. David's scribbling furiously in his notepad, guess he found something in my mother's underwear drawer. I slide around him, to spill a little tonic on his scribblings.

'Miranda!'

'Oh my, did I spill some tonic on your notebook? So sorry.' James and a few other people are sitting at the round wooden dining room table (a significant piece from the Arts and Crafts Movement) free-basing cocaine. Good to know it's useful for something. One of the women at the table has high cheekbones that meet her long brown hair in surreal right angles that are so beautiful I can't help but slump. I am as always unable to remember her name but recognize her as the new Donna Karan Icon perfume model, Icon the perfume of a generation of icons. The room has begun to fill with the pungent smell of freebase smoke, which is a pleasant change from stale cigarette smoke.

Outside, light comes from the pool.

The coke seems not to have worked, and I'm starting to feel cold, sweaty and shitty once again. But I seem to remember starting out the night feeling shitty and it's comforting knowing that I haven't gone too far with this. My body hurts, it throbs as I throw myself into an Adirondack chair.

'Can I join you?' Whit says sitting down on the chair, smoothing his bowler hat, adjusting his umbrella.

'Can I stop you?'

'You look awful.'

'Thanks, really.' I press my lips together, hard. I pull out a cigarette. He fumbles with the matches he keeps expressly to light young women's cigarettes.

'Long night? You look spent.'

'Spent?'

'Yes. You know what they're calling you, Miranda?'

'What?'

'The nineteen-year-old coke whore. That's what.'

'I don't care what people say about me.'

'Really?'

'Do you really have any blow?'

'Miranda, did you hear me? I said you are becoming a burned out coke whore. Yeah I fucked her, did her. Yeah I passed her around. Yeah, I smacked her. Yeah, she's just a whore.' There is something that changes in his face, in the inflection of his voice. I have a brief flicker of a thought that he might be right, or he might at the very least think he's right.

'Sure. Right. Uh huh.'

'And you think they'll never replace you.'

'Who could replace me? Maybe Tori Spelling could play me in the movie.'

'Shut up and listen to me. They'll replace you, replace Jeff. Nobody remembers Jeff and people liked him. His body isn't even cold.' He stops for a minute. He's wrong, I remember Jeff and that might just be enough. 'You are looking at the wrong person for sympathy. Nobody has any sympathy for you. It's hard to muster up any sympathy for someone like you. Rich kids who blow their lives on drugs. God, Randa. You're not even at the very least original.'

'Oh, that's right, you've achieved world peace.'

'Can nothing permeate your thick cocaine shell? You are a tragedy. You know that.'

'No, you don't get it. This is my party and I didn't even want you here. I didn't even invite you.' The rain is falling really hard. I motion to him that I'm going to go inside.

'See you later, Miranda.'

'Whatever.'

chapter three

A blind mention on Page Six in less than a day, now that's a party

> Just Asking – What nineteen-year-old wonder brat Jewish Nicole Kidman look-alike had a party at her socialite mother's Greenwich house? And was found freebasing in the living room far past dawn?

Maybe it says the wrong thing about me. I think I need a publicist.

What little of the house that remains is destroyed. I don't know how things got so out of hand, but then again I can't say I'm all that surprised. My mother's white carpets are obscured by gray ash from cigarettes, everything breakable from the Ming dynasty is broken. All this serves as a sure sign that the weekend's over and it's time to make another mess in some other state. I decide to pack up the hangover and go, before any of the remaining guests' tans get a chance to fade. I make a mental note to liquidate my trust fund for the purpose of paying Mom's decorator to do a fast something with the house. She has four days to do her 'magic' before Mom comes up again. But I'm sure she can find some good fabric to disguise the mess.

We get into the car and James asks and asks and asks if he can drive.

I squint; he looks like George Hamilton. 'I think I remember the last time you drove. In fact I still have nightmares about it. Your driving is Fellini, baby.'

'Do you know what a control freak you are? Do you have any idea?'

'No. No. No.' I smile as he fumbles with the back door for about fifteen minutes. Maybe I should mention the back door's broken? 'Why don't you try the other side? That door's broken.'

'Helpful.'

'Always.'

I drive too fast. Janice starts a fight with James. 'James . . . do you think it was a good idea to sell off that Calder? I mean the Principessa isn't even dead yet. The tumor still hasn't come back from the lab.' Janice and James are the ambulance chasers of the art world.

'Are you second-guessing me?' James says.

'I'm just making sure you're sure.'

'Janice. I think I know how to do this. I've been doing this since you were just a little fresh face lying naked on some billboard somewhere.' James doesn't seem like the flustered type, maybe it's because he is always somewhat flustered.

'It's just that you don't give me any authority?' I've never heard her so tentative, every one of her words ending with a question mark.

I try to stay in the lines of the West Side Highway, no small feat at a hundred-and-twenty. 'What are you talking about?' he asks, in his usual Spanish Inquisition style.

It's been suggested to me that driving is not a healthy way to express anger. I press my foot down on the accelerator until it touches the floor. The whole vehicle lurches forward. It's almost dark and only one of my headlights works.

My fingernails are cut so short that when I tap them they bleed pinkish over-exposed skin on the tight leather steering wheel. Everything feels like some war on CNN, recreated through a lens so coated with Vaseline that every dying soldier is obscured into a blurry bump running from one side of the TV screen to the other. Sometimes the blurry bumps become red, they've been hit, they blow up and sometimes the blurry bumps are just that, not soldiers, not anything, just bumps.

'You know.' She turns to him, giving him what I imagine to be a mind-fuck of a look. I accidentally turn down the radio, attempting to turn it up, to drown them out in a sea of Top Forty.

'No, what did I do this time?'

In all the years I've known Janice, I've never seen her cry, never wanted to. Now, her face crumples, grows red, folds together with every gasp, every wheeze. She's not a Glit Girl when she cries, she's ugly, the way people are when they cry. 'Forget it. Just forget it. Please.'

'Fine, we'll talk about all this later.'

'OK. Maybe you want to save this for later. Maybe you guys want to have this conversation alone.'

'Shut up.' Janice hits my seat with her fist. Not hard, but hard enough to distract me from looking at all the other drivers.

'OK,' I say, screeching off the highway at the 125th Street exit. 'I'm going to do a food shop.'

'For what?'

'Food.'

'You never buy food.'

Janice is outraged by the prospect. 'Yeah, you don't even eat. What are you going to do with food?' James says.

They seem pathetic sitting there, tan, perfectly wrinkled from an un-ironed weekend, folded in a million places.

'I think you two can get a cab on Martin Luther King Boulevard. It's only three blocks down.' Smiling, I pull into the Fairway parking lot, where all the cars in it sit neatly between the green lines drawn to keep them in place. 'Look, Fairway's having a special on ground chuck.'

'You've really lost it,' James says, trying to open the broken door.

'But I can't walk in these shoes.' Janice points to the eight-inch heel on her sneakers.

'I told you Manolo sneakers were, at the very least, ill conceived.'

'You're fucking crazy. You're high aren't you?'

'Not high enough to like you.'

Janice stumbles out of the car and down the street with James lagging behind her. She turns around in semi-shock like someone who's just seen Leo kicked out of Moomba. She waits to make sure I go into Fairway, the land of bulk-everything from a thousand rolls of toilet paper to seventeen pounds of Greek olives. That's enough olives for seventy martinis, I could drink seventy martinis in a week. That's ten martinis a day: four at lunch, two at drinks and the remaining four scattered throughout the swing clubs on the Lower East Side. I turn and wave at her when I reach the door. She just picks up her large black leather shopper and starts walking.

Fairway has long aisles, unflattering fluorescent lighting, and wonderful air-conditioner air. I gaze at myself in the long mirror over the leafy produce and imagine myself as a vegetable. How would it be to be a vegetable? A head of lettuce is so comfortable in its fate. Or is it? Doomed to become some Glit Girl's half-eaten salad, soggy, coated in oil and herbs, then slid into the trash.

I walk down the aisles; the floor's polished linoleum reflects the yellow from my dress. The store is filled with screaming children, yuppies stocking up on Diet Coke for the hectic caffeine-charged week ahead, and a scattering of strange single types buying cans of tuna and cigarettes for nights alone in front of 20/20. Every head turns to examine me in my floor-length yellow sequinned party dress.

I walk back and forth admiring all the fruits and vegetables. I grab a jar of pickles, a piece of frozen whitefish, some ham marbled with white veins of fat, and six pounds of olives for martinis. If nothing else, all of this will be an amusing topic of conversation later.

The cashier wears a red polyester vest. She looks over her plastic name tag at me. I press my lips together. She looks up from the package of ham, with dark brown eyes. I almost think she asks me if I'm OK. But when I look at her as if to say 'No, I'm not OK. I need . . .' she just tells me it'll be twelve ninety-five for that, and I'm holding up the line.

Back in the car, I cruise along the highway, thinking about Death. My mother's best friend died last year, electrocuted by a high-voltage facial. I try to imagine what she looked like with her hair burnt at the roots; everything biodegraded except her silicone, which will probably outlive her great-grandchildren. Mom was devastated, but I always knew electricity wasn't the answer to good skin. My cell phone rings.

'You wanna go to a party?' If I had a dollar for every time . . .

'Hi, Brett. Aren't I on my way home from a party?' I smile, light a cigarette and almost hit a gypsy cab.

'Great! So then it's not like you're going to a new party at all, more like you're just stopping somewhere on your way home.'

'Brett, your logic astounds me. You should be a doctor.'

'That's just what my mother says.'

'Go figure.'

'You have your car. Pick me up.'

'Unlikely.'

'Why not?'

'I have issues with parallel parking.'

'Come on . . . meet me outside Gitane.'

'Fine, Brett. Fine. But if we die in a car crash it's not my fault.'

'Is it ever your fault?'

It's one of those nights, late July in SoHo, when it's too hot to walk and you can't remember ever having a goal in your life. Brett is waiting out front. He doesn't see me. I honk the horn. He waves at me, but I keep honking the horn because I want to. He smiles and starts walking toward the car.

A woman walks by our exchange. She seems to have been pulled directly out of central casting for her ability to look thin in gingham. She smiles. Brett grins back at the girl. I lean down on the horn.

'Brett!' I scream through the air conditioning and closed windows.

'What, Miranda? I heard you the first time with the horn. Give it a rest.' He opens the passenger door and climbs in.

'So, gorgeous. How are you doing?'

'Good.' Brett leans over to hug me. He smells of cherry flavored chapstick, other people's cigarettes, and Secret deodorant. I kiss him on the lips and linger there for a minute; maybe that will erase his memory of smiley Miss Gingham. 'I brought you some food.' He places a white paper bag on my lap.

'Why?' The car behind me starts to honk. I think of the whitefish probably already rotting in the trunk.

'By my calculations you haven't eaten in two days.' I open the bag. It's filled with bread-y things: a wholewheat roll slathered in butter, a shiny sticky bun, a brown bagel.

'What do you want me to do with this stuff?' The cars behind me continue to honk. I step on the gas.

'Why don't you eat it? Come on, Randa, this is hardly rocket science.'

'Fine.' I pull out the bagel and take a bite. The dry bagel chokes me. I try to cough.

'I guess it's been a while since I've eaten.' Is it possible I've forgotten how to eat?

There is this feeling trapped in the humid air, this feeling of guiltless laziness. This feeling that even if I wanted to work, my work would be fruitless. Maybe it's the heat that has killed my ambition.

'You're crazy.' Brett plays with the leftover carbs. He takes a bite of the sticky bun. Brett doesn't know crazy.

'Do you think I'm a good person?'

'What?' He doesn't look up at me. He's busy pulling nuts off the bun.

'Do you think I'm a decent human being?'

'When has that ever been your goal, Miranda?' he asks between chews.

'What are you talking about? That space's big enough for a city bus. It's practically the whole block.'

'I know, but.' I drive past the space. 'I don't know how to parallel park.'

'Yeah, but that's hardly parallel parking that's just pulling in.'

'I don't know how to parallel park. Do I need to say it again?'

'How did you get your license?'

'Did I say I had a license?'

'God, Miranda.'

'What? I trust myself enough to not have a license. That's just a legal technicality anyway.'

'There's nothing to do with you.' He seems melancholy, annoyingly so. 'Do you think about Jeff?'

'Sure.'

'Do you think about him a lot?'

'Yeah.'

'I'm going to stop doing cocaine.' Brett says, not looking at me.

'But you hardly do it now. You need to have a habit to quit a habit.'

'You have a habit.' He puts his small sweaty hand over mine.

'I would say, I have a little more than a habit.'

Brett sometimes thinks he is a doctor. He sometimes thinks he can offer some great insight into my drug habit, but the truth is that frosting mattresses is a far cry from removing bullets with a scalpel in the ER.

'Listen, Dr Brett, let me suggest that you are not a doctor, not even a podiatrist.'

Brett is eight years older than I am. He thinks that gives him some kind of authority to lecture me about my little problem. But him being old doesn't mean anything. It certainly doesn't make him smarter than I am, nor does it make him saner than I am. He's covered in sticky nuts from the sticky bun.

I pull forward to line up with the car in front of us.

'Get out.'

'What?'

'Get out of the car. I'll park it for you.'

'Fine.' I get out of the car and stand on the sidewalk.

If I were a self-conscious person, possessing the kind of self-obsessed neurosis that is marked by paranoia, I would be embarrassed to stand by helplessly while my ex-boyfriend parked my car. But all I can really think is that Brett seems to have always been my ex-boyfriend, so much so I can't remember ever dating him. I look at Brett, struggling to make the steering wheel go in his direction. His perfect sin is eating pork. We could never agree.

Brett's got cocaine sewn into the pockets of his suit like he might have sewn gold into his pockets a hundred years before. It's a mystery how he can afford to support my habit, but who cares? All that matters is that he does.

We go to some British dilettante's SoHo loft. I do some coke and Brett social climbs and before I know it, I've lost yet another night, it's gone.

It's five a.m. when I come to semi-consciousness again.

'Who are you, again? I'm sorry but I'm bad with names, bad with names and faces, or both.' I say, somewhat dazed. To the guy I realize I've probably been talking to for some time but I can't remember.

'Will Shearwolf, the Third. Very nice. Very nice. Yes.' A little Darwin, please bear with me here: Brit trumps heroin addict; heroin addict trumps celebrity, except The Donald; and everyone trumps socialite.

'That's right. I know you.' Small red-faced Will Shearwolf with the shiny head married his mother's best friend when he found out she was worth ten billion dollars. Now his mother's dead, her best friend's dead, and Will's blowing through seventeen-year-old Russian models like they're going out of style.

'Nice to.' I reach out my shaky right hand and am met with a clammy British one. '. . . meet you.'

He has a slightly mushy face like the faces on Mount Rushmore rereated in melting chopped liver. A face that is proof of the tendency of society's highest echelon to inbreed. 'So, Miss Miranda. What's the news?'

'I don't know. But I'm sure I can find out what the P.W.A.P.P. are doing.'

'Who?'

'The P.W.A.P.P., people who are past their prime, grist for the glue factory, my friends. Possibly you've heard of them. So, how do you know me?' I love the rush of ego I get when people remember me. I'm no shrink, but I've clocked enough hours with one to postulate this could be the product of feeling invisible.

'I know everything. You introduced yourself to me five times in the last hour.' I stare at his little square glasses, at the crosses that lie on his face, formed by the light and his glasses.

'Quite a burden, knowing everything, don't you think?'

'You know, Miss Miranda . . . can I call you Randa?' He's loud British and drunk, but of course I'm JAPPY obnoxious and high, so I'm not really in the position to judge.

'No.' I take a quick glance into my handbag, keys (now if only I could remember where I live), gum (sugar-free of course), wallet, lipstick (Metallic Vamp by Chanel), eye shadow, Clorets, and coke. Hum, no coke. Where's the coke? 'Excuse me for a second, Bill.'

'It's Will.'

'Like I care.' I say under my breath. I walk away, inspecting my environment. The walls of the loft, are dark, almost black. They are lit with red lights, and the air is a Chex Party Mix of smoke from everything that can be smoked and the usual unmasked summer B.O. The room is filled with sweaty people who have gotten more attractive in direct proportion to the night's intake of booze and drugs.

I look around the room for anyone who looks even vaguely familiar, but the sad truth is everyone looks familiar because everyone looks the same: dismay on their faces, polished clothing in all the most vivid shades of black, blow-dried hair, a pocket full of rise-printed business cards with some profession scrawled across the bottom, and a half-lit cigarette hanging out of their mouths. Then I see James. Two problems killed with one stone in one person: someone I can talk to and someone with coke.

'What's that coming out of your nose?'

I look down at my hand.

'Blood.'

I lean over James, to kiss him hello. Some blood

falls on his fingers. He grimaces and frantically tries to wipe the blood off his hand. He hands me his used Kleenex. I'm coming down fast, and for a moment I think all my life might be about fear and emptiness, each taking their turn with me.

'Hey, James.' I turn to him. The coke left in my underwear drawer isn't going to be enough to get me through tomorrow at the dreaded gallery.

I had thought I had done a fairly good job of getting rid of Will or Bill or whatever he thinks his name is, but clearly not a good enough job, because here he is sauntering up to us with a half smirk, half smile that could only mean one thing: he's here to admire James' cleft chin.

'What's the matter, baby?' James kisses me on the top of my head. 'Who's your friend? You look so pale.' I sit down on one of the peach bordello chairs, crossing my stubbly legs.

'Oh, yeah. Sorry. Yeah . . . That's right. My friend Will Shearwolf. Will, meet Janice's husband, James.' James frowns, like I should have known not to mention that he's legally married. 'James, meet Will.'

'A pleasure.' James extends a hand to Will. Will smiles at James like he wants to fuck him. Be my guest, I'll just find some place to lay down and die.

'Miranda, are you OK?' James stops. 'Do you need to go to after hours?' he whispers.

'How did you know?' I pinch my nose to keep the blood from falling onto my yellow sequinned dress.

The only thing that might work at a time like this is the most desperate of measures: chasing the dragon. I reach into my blue handbag, recently stolen from a distracted Hermes salesgirl busy selling my mother thick plaid wool summer sweaters. I unzip the zipper and pull out a glass pipe. This'll make me feel a little better. I pack a little heroin in the bowl. Smoking heroin after snorting coke is a bit like having a Tasti-DLite on the way home from the gym.

Will comes charging over. 'No, you . . . can't do that . . . not here. WHAT DO YOU THINK THIS IS SOME KIND OF CRACK DEN?'

'A heroin den?'

Then, as if right on cue in a moment of pure stage direction, James and Will each grab one of my arms and walk me out of the party. Actually they're walking and I'm being dragged.

'Where are we going? After hours?' I yell.

'Would you shut up?' James says twisting my arm behind my shoulder.

'Ow.'

Brett's talking to a small girl with a short pug face and a mane of red hair. She's dressed in a skirt that reveals the cellulite on her butt and upper thighs. She and I look at each other like predatory animals fighting for food in the wild. I'm much thinner than she is but I'm crazy, so if she's anywhere near sane her score is probably a 4 for face, 1 for body, 4 for sanity, whereas I probably break down to something like this: 4 for face, 4 for body,

O for sanity = 8 overall, with an especially low score for personality. But having no personality doesn't really seem to make any kind of visible difference at NYC parties.

'What are you looking at, flabby bitch.' I say.

'Nothing.' She says, turning back to Brett. I realize she's probably right. What's another fallen institution anyway? Just further proof that children of famous people are like communism – better in concept than in practice.

chapter four

Let's play the suicide game. Let me explain how, then you can do it at home with me. It's easy. Try to think of all the possible ways to commit suicide in alphabetical order. A-Absolut vodka drunk to the point of alcohol poisoning; B-bb gun; C-choking on a cheese sandwich; D-drug overdose; E-electrocution; F-set myself on fire; G-ground down by taxi; H-too much heroin; I-incineration, and so on.

I'm eating a Prozac power bar; what a great idea mixing psychopharmacology with food, whoever thought? Maybe later on I'll have a Pepto-Bismol brownie. I'm drunk on martini olives or the vodka in the martini, hard to know which one. The chocolate Prozac crumbs get all over my authentic seventies purple plastic poncho, the one Mom wore at Woodstock or Gstaad. Another four-hour lunch hour is over, leaving three hours of workday, that is assuming what I do is considered work.

I get to West Broadway and I'm on S. S-Sleeping

with the fishes in the Hudson, but I lost the card for the hit man I used to date. I push open the glass door, slip on the super-slick white floor and try to slide behind the desk before anyone notices I've been at lunch for four hours.

There's no furniture anywhere. Then again, who needs furniture? Of course a little furniture might be useful, but there's nothing in the six gallery rooms except for my desk and my chair. On the walls is 'kitsch' from floor to ceiling in all shades of neon.

This is it, the last frontier of employment for the low functioning: professionally sitting behind the desk at an art gallery. Essentially getting paid to smoke and give out dirty looks, which is something I'd do for free. My days are filled with the mystery of what it is I'm waiting for. Maybe it's for some saint to come in and buy something, anything. Please.

At six o'clock, all of us desk-waiters mix, go to art openings, sleep with each other, and talk about how famous we're going to be. Famous for what? Good question. But there is no answer. On any given night there will be as many as thirty art openings, all filled with the same people, the same art, all with open bars with the same vodka.

Peter Dean has openings in Chelsea. Usually it's a packed room filled with high desk-waiters who couldn't buy his art because they don't even have health insurance. A desk-waiter, as I see it, is usually one of two things: a trust fund-er looking for something to have on the bottom of a business card a.k.a. ME, or an aspiring artist looking for an In. Now there is one problem with being a desk-waiter, it's a step below gutting fish at a fish market; also, people who gut fish make more money.

Where Peter Dean may be the TNBT-lite, my boss, Kandy Macmillan, is an old cow, and I say that in the nicest possible way. Ah, what does it matter saving face, she hates me anyway. I take four-hour lunches, not exactly making me the most productive employee.

Robin, who is almost as low-paid as I am, comes by the desk to give me a sheet of slides to file. She leans over me. There is something passively bossy about little Miss split-ends. 'You smell like booze.'

'That's because I've been drinking.'

'Have an Altoid, she wants to speak with you.' She points up the stairs to Kandy's office. Through the glass door I can see her tight bun of grey hair and the hot pink desk where the 'magic' happens.

'Sit!' Kandy is known for her charm.

'You wanted to see me?'

Kandy's a small square woman. She used to be an actress until she married (let's say snagged) a rich guy. After snagging him, she killed him with a butter and hollandaise overdose. Then she took his money and became old money almost overnight. Her voice is deep from smoking too many butchy brown cigarettes; when she speaks she sounds like Howard Coselle. To sum up, Kandy's a nouveau socialite in the worst way.

'Is that what you're wearing to the opening?' Her eyes move over my poncho, a whimsical selection, picked out by Dina, everyone's favorite bipolar personal shopper.

'I guess not.' Maybe Dina didn't take her Depacoat that day.

'That outfit just seems . . .'

'Mother, did you call?'

'Look at Miranda. Robert, what's wrong with her?'

'Ohhh, you have a point, don't you, Mother.' My mother always feebly hoped that one day I would marry Robert, but I don't think Robert ever hoped he'd marry me.

Robert was briefly engaged to Janet Halstone, sole heir to the single largest toilet paper fortune in the world, and for a few months every time they bought a pint of milk, *ETC* was there chronicling whether it was skim or whole. Then the mentions started, like little red bricks, on Page six:

' . . . an heiress and a social worker, spending long afternoons at the Four Seasons. Seems that she's getting well-er on the bed, as opposed to the couch.'

We all knew it was Janet, and soon after she officially got rid of Robert for the natty social worker. She fell out of our world into some suburban land of frozen vegetables and lawn mowers. All this made Robert slightly less eligible. A cuckold – and there was no amount of handmade shoes that could reverse that very fact.

As I start down the stairs, I can feel his heavy feet behind me.

'Miranda.'

'Yes.' I continue down.

'What's the menu for tonight?'

'Ask someone who eats.' We arrive at the bottom of the steps.

'You know, I was thinking I should ask you out.'

I see him inspecting himself in the mirror. I walk to my desk and sit down.

'Write on this.' He hands me some paper.

'What?'

'Your phone number, that's what.' I write a number on the piece of paper.

'See you, gorgeous. I'll call you later.' Not likely, because I gave him my mother's fax number.

I spend the rest of the afternoon trying to get my nose to clot and reading *Mavda* magazine, which is so hip I can't read the type face.

The waiters and bartenders swarm around like locusts, setting up for the party. They ask me where things are, and if they can use the phone, and if I can help them with the lock on the bathroom door. My stock answer is No. It works OK.

When they approach me again, I pretend not to speak English, which makes it tricky to answer the phone. At five minutes to five, Robin walks down the stairs, offers me a Berlitz language guide, and tells me it's not OK not to answer the phone. Fortunately, she also announces that if we don't go get drunk soon she's going to quit. She's always threatening to quit, but she can't quit because she's the only one who knows where the slides are, and what they're of.

We casually jet down Mercer Street, leaving Kandy alone with the caterers and the bathroom door that won't lock.

'Four vodka martinis very dry, three olives,' I say to Steve the bartender/painter. Now that I do coke all day long, I find my drinking is not as extreme as it used to be. He lines up the martinis one in front of the other. I love the idea of going through a row of martinis, one after another after another.

'So, how's my favorite socialite princess?' Steve asks as he offers me some bar nuts. A tribe of Pygmies can live for a month off the caloric content of one handful of bar nuts.

'Not to . . . ' Should I be insulted?

Steve and I then have the kind of conversation that could make your brain fall out, a sort of half flirt, half network kind of thing in the ugliest way – lots of me squealing and giggling like a pig in heat.

Robin emerges from the bathroom, we both drink until there are two Steves.

Kandy is furious when we stumble back into the gallery. The party has already started. I'm quite drunk. Shouldn't have had that fourth martini.

Kandy is standing by the door, greeting the battalion of bulimics as they come in with their checkbooks and leave with pieces of hot pink condiments masquerading as Art. Art, what a mistake. Kandy leans over me, her breath smells like one too many pre-party glasses of red wine.

'Where the hell have you been?'

She grabs my arm, instructs me not to talk and walks me over to a well-dressed art type. 'Miranda, meet Julian.' I reach out my hand to a man who looks genuinely uninterested in me. 'Miranda's father is Jason Woke, THE ARCHITECT, and Miranda's mother is Diana Camdinsky, THE SOCIALITE.' It's as if she's reading my resumé to him. 'And her grandfather is Simon Woke, THE COMMUNIST PLAYWRIGHT.' The dignity is being drained out of me with every second that passes.

Some writer from *Art News* comes up to the Schnozzle to ask for his opinion on post modernism. Schnozzle walks away without so much as a look. I move to the other side of the room where I pour myself a nice stiff vodka in a plastic glass.

The greasy haired 'talent' stands alone, lodged between two pieces of undigested birthday cake, in her designer dress, cradling her mailing list like a newborn child. I would use the word talent loosely. Why is it that all you have to do is smell to be considered a great painter in the art world? I stick a cigarette in my mouth and realize that I don't have a lighter.

'Shit.'

'Is there a problem?' Robert holds his grey and gold lighter up to my cigarette. Robert has big wobbly wrinkly hands, the hands of a sixty-year-old unhappily placed on a thirty-year-old. I like a man with liver spots. It's sexy, and it reminds me of my grandfather.

'Solved by your chivalry.'

'I want to take you to dinner.'

'Wow, does that mean you'll pay?'

'Yes it means I'll pay.'

'Tonight?'

'If you can?'

'I'll go get my cardigan.' I head to the bathroom. The walls are covered with orange graffiti by a Basquiat wannabe, who never happened. The light bulb flickers, it's on its way to going dead. I open the door and slip into stall numero uno and dump out my leftover cocaine. Only two grams; there's no way I can last on this. With one hand, I dial Brett's number on my cell phone and with the other hand I cut up the remaining cocaine into lines, which I snort while singing my high school's anthem, ' . . . 'tis the spirit that quicken-ith or sinken-ith,' Five . . . Six . . . Seven . . . Eight. I snort the first three lines. I liked my high school. Maybe that was the best life is ever going to be?

'Miranda?' Brett's voice sounds sharp.

'How did you know it was me.'

'Who else would answer the phone snorting.' I laugh, and he doesn't.

'Would you do me a favor?'

'Anything.'

I inspect a hairball in the drain.

'Drop off some candy for me.'

'What?'

'I'm having dinner with Robert Macmillan and I need some strychnine.'

'Dinner, like a date?'

'No, business.' I snort the rest of the lines, as I apply powder to my nose.

'No.'

'Come on, Brett. Please.'

'Fine. But never ever again.'

'Great.'

'This is the last time.'

'Meet you in front of the Brasserie in twenty minutes – and whatever you do don't come in.'

'And my mother said you treat me badly.'

'Oh and Brett . . .'

'Yeah?'

'Thanks.'

'Sure, Miranda.'

One more phone call for insurance. 'Hello, Janice? This is Randa.'

'Yeah what?' She's annoyed.

'Where are you?'

'Who knows.'

'Will you come to the Brasserie? I have a little dream date with this guy, Robert Macmillan. I need a little dope.'

'Whatever. How much is it worth to you?'

'A lot.'

'Two hundred dollars?'

'Sold.'

Hanging up the phone, I wipe the little white half-moons of cocaine off my nostrils.

Robert is standing by the wall and I can see from the expression on his face that I've been gone a little too long.

'Trouble finding your sweater?' He laughs.

'Yeah.'

The Brasserie has only been open for three months. It shines of the usual New York City grime, Page Six grime, *Observer* grime, Euro grime, oily fish grime, and grimy brass fixtures. As soon as we walk in I feel my shoulders slump forward; this place makes my posture suck. A very rude, very French maitre d' seats us at a small white marble table by the window, lodged between Chity Mc-chit-chit, the famed Italian porn star, and Kary Bee Greenberg, the unsuccessful politician and handbag designer. He orders a screwdriver and I order three double vodka martinis straight up, very dry with three olives in each.

He's glossy like a movie star and wispy like a librarian. He leans forward like he's going to tell me he's always been in love with me. 'Randa, I think it's important that you know I'm not into you at all.'

'Thanks.'

'No really.' He sips. 'I think at nineteen you've

already been around the block a few too many times.'

'I guess.' There's got to be an olive in the bottom of this martini glass if I could just find it.

'Also I'm gay.'

'YEAH, well . . . You're gay?'

He sips some more of his drink, I try to drown in mine. 'What's the matter, babe, am I the first gay person you've ever met in the art world? Am I, babe?'

'Why call me babe? That assumes affection.'

'This is why people think you're such a bitch.'

'So far this is tons of fun.'

'What's wrong with you?' He's suddenly concerned.

'Nothing.'

'Are you sure? You look awful.'

'This dinner sure is an ego booster. So I might as well tell you that I'm a cocaine addict.' Then it starts, the dripping. I casually put my finger on my nostril. I am not the least bit surprised when it comes back coated with blood. Robert looks horrified. I excuse myself into the bathroom, no sign of Brett.

A heavy brown door guards the entrance to one of the premiere coke-snorting bathrooms in all of New York City. The bathroom is what the owners imagine a brasserie bathroom to be: red and white tiles, yellow brass fixtures, and small round mirrors. It is my favorite stall bathroom in this city.

There are three categories of bathroom in New York City – The Doorless Stall, The Stall, and The Room. Privacy makes The Room far superior to either kind of stall. All that said, this bathroom has its perks and for them I think of it as a stall-plus. This bathroom is perfect for drugs, clean enough to feel sterile, small enough to feel private, and used by lots of drug addicts every day. By that token, Star Coffee on Astor Place is the best place to shoot dope, because so many people use it to get off – it's like the neighborhood personal shooting gallery. This way you never feel like you're breaking any rules, although I never feel like I'm breaking any rules anyway, because I have this thing the shrinks like to call flexible morality or borderline personality disorder.

Janice got here as promised, but what she's doing in the bathroom and not in the bar is a mystery to me. She seems fascinated by the dirty round mirror over the sink as if it could provide some answers. She doesn't look that great under the yellow fluorescent light. She doesn't look that great when she rolls up her sleeve to show me she's collapsed every vein in her left arm.

'It's a silicone jungle out there.'

'Hey, Miranda. What's going on? Where's the money? Wasn't it clever of me to wait for you in the bathroom instead of the bar?'

'Yeah, you're a rocket scientist.' I hand her some cash.

'Thanks. I won't count it, 'cause I trust you.' She winks, pushing up her sleeve.

'Shit Janice, what the hell is wrong with your arm?'

'What isn't.' She pushes the garbage can in front of the door. 'Do you think this'll work?'

'For what?' I say, still horrified by her bruised arm. 'To keep people from coming in. God, for someone from a family of geniuses, you seem to have missed the genetic boat.'

'Right.'

'Pretty bad? You think?' She points to the track marks down her arm. She rolls up her other sleeve, the other arm is worse. I gag. Between big red bumps, there are spots of ooze, pus, dried blood, and dirt. It looks like she hasn't washed her arm in months.

'I would say, why don't you shower?'

'Never shoot dope.'

I watch her slide down to the floor, lean on the wall. She doesn't say anything to me, which I'm glad about. It's nearly impossible to have a conversation with someone who's tying off. She lights the lighter under the spoon and slides her hands down her black dress. She pulls the belt off her waist and wraps it around her arm.

She slides her hands up and down her arms looking for a vein. She can't find one. Panicking, she moves her hands faster, sliding them, making grunting sounds, tying and untying the tourniquet, you can see it in her eyes the moment she realizes she can shoot dope into her neck.

'Great.' She's so happy to find a large plump vein, one that's plump enough to use. She's down on the floor now, trying to get all the angles right.

The powder police are knocking on the bathroom door, as if the shine of their noses would make it impossible for them to digest their oysters.

She's started to look old for thirtyish, not having any more veins. All the moguls and models of her age have crossed over, leaving Janice alone in the world of the S P (the Single People), a pack of panicky premenopausal predatory Prada-wearing paradoxes looking for the 40 carats that mark a debut in *The New York Times* Wedding Section. She might have been the girl everyone looked at five years ago, but now she doesn't exist anymore; having fallen through the cracks gracelessly, she's been dismissed from the list.

Janice gazes up at me with her exotic almond-shaped eyes, the only thing left from her days as an It girl. Still sweating, she comes back long enough to offer me a full syringe. I lift my left leg and present her with my calf. She dips the needle under my skin. I've got you under my skin, deep in the heart of me . . .

I don't like needles too much, making me a somewhat unsuccessful heroin addict. But the needle doesn't hurt half as much as the heroin, burning, ripping through the veins, and then in a second or two it passes and the burning is replaced

with that beautiful delicious downward floating
feeling.

'Janice, I love you.'

'Oh, baby. I know that, honey. I love you too . . .
'She reaches up over the sink and starts to vomit.
The women are now screaming at the top of their
little surgically enhanced lungs to get into the
bathroom, but all that doesn't seem to matter any
more. 'I think . . .' Her head comes up slowly. Her
face is covered with vomit, her voice filled with
uncomfortable twitches and intermissions of
thought.

'Yeah?' But then I start to fall and it's too late
cause I'm throwing up too and something is swal-
lowing me.

*'Miranda.' Jeff is standing behind me, making my
blinking and everything else that is part of me, stop. He
stops me with his heavy breath, each gasp freezing me
deeper.*

*I don't remember his chin being so sharp, or his eyes
being so far sunken in. Seeing him makes me realize
how little of him I remember. I thought I knew him, the
slope of his cheeks and the way his lips meet each other
under his nose, rounded like arches. I didn't think time
could take away what felt so burnt into me. His skin
white as Elmer's Glue or horse bones. He stands with his
hands in the pockets of his brown jeans, like there is
nothing I could do that would ever impress him.*

*He is the most popular boy in school and he loves me,
only me, or so he says every minute of the day. He drives
the best car and has the coolest friends and kisses me*

right in the middle of my neck were the skin goes in. And he makes me feel special in a way that I won't ever feel again, now that he's dead.

There is something very right about this, him on one side of death, me on the other. Both of us knowing the loneliness may kill me before the drugs ever have their chance.

Robert's here, screaming something at me. I can't understand anything he's saying because there's a big space between him and me. I try to tell him that I don't think I'm gonna make it to any more parties tonight.

In fact I have a feeling I may not make it at all.

chapter five

chapter five

Maybe last night wasn't a triumphant moment in the Woke family history, or here's an even sicker thought, maybe it was. After all, one card-carrying member of the A-list (Kandy's son Robert) and one ex-boyfriend (Brett) carried me home, up the stairs and into my apartment. When Kandy's son Robert did the deed, carried me up the steps in my valiant return home from the Brasserie, all I could hear in my half fog was him complaining about how much I weigh.

'She's so heavy. Can't we just leave her here?'

I think I'd be OK if I could just quit smoking, three packs of Camel not-so-lights would make anyone feel shitty.

When Brett goes into the bathroom I knock back three of my emergency Valiums and some dust bunnies from the lining of my jacket pocket. 'What are you doing in there, shaving your back hair?' He doesn't respond, but I hear a razor.

I start to fall asleep and accidentally sock Brett in the eye with my watch. He clutches his eye and yelps. I turn over and hit him with my other arm. He mumbles, 'I hope the Valium kicks in soon.'

It's dark out when I wake up. I have such a profound thirst that four liters of brown tap water seem negligible. The headache I've acquired is so torturous the only recourse I can think of is seven Aleve.

When I wake up again, it's still dark, and the headache has returned; it's vengeful, causing me to make a mad fumble through the dresser for something stronger than Aleve.

8:23 a.m. Alarm rings. Time for work or pork buns.

9:24 a.m. Brett gets up and turns off alarm.

Brett says he has to go home. When I come to, it's light out. I get up and faint.

I realize that I haven't eaten in a while so I order pork buns, charging them to Brett's Visa that is in the wallet he has kindly forgotten and left on my bureau. Then I lie on my red-and-white striped sofa, coming down, waiting for the pork buns to arrive.

It is out of boredom that I flip on the TV. 'Melrose Place' sings into my ear, a little too loud. I drop a lit cigarette on the sofa and watch the smoke rise; drugs have, if nothing else, given me a delayed reaction time. I don't get to the flames until yet another blond-lette falls into Melrose Place's communal swimming pool. The pool makes me remember my mandatory bottle of hangover water that sits on my desk. I reach for it and douse my flaming sofa.

When the phone rings, the fire is out, my. headache is gone and I'm back thinking of ways to kill myself. Strychnine, codeine, Valium . . .

'Miranda Woke?'

'This is she.' Ever the grammarian.

'This is Jenny.' She pauses. 'Your stepmother.'

'Ohh, Hi.'

'Hi.' My father is considered a catch, good looking – for a short, fat, balding Jewish man who's rich, rich, rich, and famous, famous, famous – the Frank Lloyd Wright of his generation and not gay, not that I know of anyway. I hear a man's voice in the background, I lean into the receiver. 'Your father and I are in town for just one night and I, I mean he, thought it would be great if you might meet us at this opening for P.S. 1.'

'I would love to.'

'Fine.' My father's new young British thing (stepmonster number five) is twenty-two. That makes her three years older than I am.

'Maybe . . . we can get some dinner after?'

'Maybe, we'll see. Definite maybe,' she says.

'Is he there? Can I speak to him?'

'I hear her put the phone down and mutter some words across the room. 'Miranda. He's really busy. But he says he'll see you there. We'll send a car to pick you up.'

'Can I just—'

'Are you still in that apartment on Eighth Street?'

'Yeah.'

'The car should pick you up around six. Look for a green Mercedes.'

'Jenny.'

'What?' From the sound of her voice, it's clear to me my father has made her old, or older than when I first met her.

'Nothing.'

I put down the empty receiver and walk over to the liquor cabinet, take the half-empty bottle of Smirnoff, and empty it into my mouth.

When the pork buns arrive, they are cold, pink, and undercooked.

I can't remember inviting Janice over but it doesn't really matter if I invited her or not. The truth is she'd show up sooner or later. She looks blurry, dressed in grey sweater material: She mutters something, as she drops an eightball on the coffee table. Before I can ask her what the hell she's talking about, she's asleep. I check to make sure she's still breathing. Three cigarettes later she's as still as Lake Placid, prompting me to check for a pulse. Half a gram of blow later, Janice turns over and vomits all over the sofa – a good sign for her, but not for the furniture. I think it might be time for a new couch.

I look down at my watch, which is set twenty minutes fast to offset my cocaine lateness, or is it twenty minutes slow, or thirty minutes fast?

In honor of my father, I decide to wear something fresh from the dry cleaner, my favorite black dress. I slip the dress over my head. I love that fresh from the dry cleaner smell.

The driver buzzes. Janice gets up and slinks into the bathroom.

I look out the window to check if the car is waiting outside. All those people walking up and down Eighth Street look so normal. I wonder how they do it. 'Janice.' I look back out the window. 'Janice.' Maybe normality isn't a goal, but being able to leave the house certainly is. 'JANICE. Let's go. Please.' I pound on the door.

Janice comes out of the bathroom, slides her hand into mine, pulls me into the elevator, and eventually into the waiting car.

My favorite Manhattan activity has to be sitting in traffic. It's by far the most spiritually fulfilling, able to give a good procuration conversation a run for the money. The procuration conversation goes something like this: 'I went to blank store and bought blank item, which I read about in blank magazine, which I know blank celebrity also owns/wears. By the way, the item cost blank amount of dollars, isn't that a deal?' It almost always isn't.

Janice offers me a sip from what is supposedly her hip flask, but on closer inspection is actually my hip flask with my initials on it. Because I'm high, bored, and feel like it, I start screaming at her.

By the time we arrive at the old public school, now a museum, on the wrong side of the

Midtown Tunnel, we are both in a kind of no-talking zone.

We pull up to a paparazzi line, and enter the lying-to-each-other zone. 'Umm, you look great, too. I mean it. You look really great, too.' And surprisingly, she does look great, in a tight black dress that shows she has zero percent body fat, actually she looks fantastic for someone who shoots enough heroin to kill a horse every day. Unfortunately she doesn't talk that great, lately every word that comes out of her mouth is in Swahili; you need a decoder ring to ask her where the bathroom is.

'Thanks, you look good, too. Oh look there's Schnozzle.' She gathers herself and swings her narrow hips into the crowd leaving me alone, to walk and talk alone. 'Hi, Debra.' Smile at Debra. 'Hi, Delia.' Wave . . . wave. 'Hi, Candice.' Smirk at Candice. 'Hi, Cynthia.' The famous guy passes on my left and I snag him by the sleeve. 'Hey, the famous guy.' Roger at five o'clock. 'How are you, Roger?' A mass of blond hair jogs by. 'What's going on, Kerry?' An older gentleman. 'Hello, Frank.' An ex-boyfriend. 'Hey, John.' A pair of glasses attached to a face. 'What's going on, Bill?' Small and dark. 'Hi, Samantha.' Tall and dark. 'Hey, Lizabeth.' On the left, the left, grab her arm and MMMAAA 'How are you, Cindy?' A grade school friend, 'What's going on, Rory?' Another young artist. 'Nice to see you, Amy. Miranda Woke. Remember me?' An old actress. 'You lost weight, Kate. Nice to see you.' On the right, grab her arm, she shrugs off me. 'Hey, Mari.' Multiple piercing. 'Hey, Mike.'Twenty-nine-year-old power curator. 'How are you, Sarah?' Multiple tattoos. 'Good to see you, Sabrina.' A fashion designer. 'How are you, Christian?' A fashion designer. 'Hey, Andy.' A family friend.

'Laura Goldstein.' The whitefish princess blocks my path to the bar. Nobody blocks my path to the bar.

'It's me, Laura. Remember me?' Laura Goldstein, daughter of Sam Goldstein the whitefish king of New York, may have looked like a whitefish at one time. But clearly the profits from twenty-dollar-a-pound whitefish sales financed a few minor adjustments to whitefish Laura. Adjustments like hair, nose, cheeks, a course in speaking Upper East Side-isms (gorgeous-darling-let's-go-to-Fred's-for-a-few-leaves), a Filofax the size of *The Satanic Verses*, and the mandatory jewelry modeling job at an auction house on lower Fifth Avenue. Thanks to her surgeon, Laura no longer looks like a sturgeon.

'Ohh, hi.'

'Miranda Woke. How are you?'

'I'm great. Fab. Amazing. Working a lot on a million different things. My God, I am so busy. It's amazing how busy I am. Beyond busy. So busy my God.'

'Gee that is so-o-o great. Did you see your father? He's here you know.'

'No, not yet but I'm sure he's waiting for me somewhere. Me and dad, we're so tight you know. Gosh, gotta find him. What are you looking at? Is there something in my teeth?'

'Don't worry. There's nothing in your teeth.'

'Oh my God, work is going so well. Did I tell you how well? I bet Dad's in the VIP room, waiting for his little girl.'

She nods, somewhat befuddled by my high-speak (fast cocaine talk).

'Oh, I know, know, know. Do I know? I'm in the know.'

'He put you on the list?'

'Laura, Laura, Laura, are you joking? Of course he put me on the list. I *am* the fucking list.'

'Well, if not, I can probably help. But it's a hard room tonight; Partha Dewart, decorator to the stars, and Pawn Snuffy Bones, the rap star are here. There's really tight security and as always . . .' She stops and sighs, like maybe she's been to too many parties this lifetime. 'It's all really badly organized, so it's really going be a feat of my genius to get you into the VIP room.'

'Whatever, whatever. I'm on the list, so don't lose any sleep over it.'

'I know. But you know how these things work, Randa. I mean really.'

'Laura, Laura, Laura, can we talk about this later? I really need to go.'

'If you have any problems with the list or anything.'

'I'm absolutely, positively not the slightest bit worried, at all, ever. I cut my teeth on these things, trust me I know what to do.'

'Sure, sure, Miranda. While you're waiting you should go check out the giant cow if you get a chance. It's called the Sacred Cow and it's hanging from the ceiling on the second floor. It's amazing – it's alive and everything. Ohh here's an invite for the after party.' She hands me an invite. 'We're doing it BBQ style, Sacred Cow burgers and soy pups. Did I mention I've become a vegan?'

She kisses me and goes off to meet her whitefish prince.

No sight of Dad, but I'm hyper aware of Peter Dean standing ten feet in front of me. I watch him scan the room for money or fame and then gradually decide that I'm important enough to speak to, though I have no idea why.

'Miranda.' Piranha teeth extend in a way that's charming, young art dealers have little baby teeth, for sucking up small trust funds that belong to young collectors.

'Yeah what? What's up Dean?' Who names their child Dean?

'You look like you're coming down.'

'Always.'

'I can fix that for you Miranda Woke. I can *fix* that.' He winks.

'Can you?'

'Sure.' He nods to me.

He always gives me free coke because he thinks

I'm going to buy art from him. This might not be the best way to drive business, after all don't coke heads just want more coke? What would I do with his art, with a giant inflatable fish covered in honey mustard, unless I could smoke it?

I get dizzy looking down the steps. He pulls out a set of odd Victorian keys. I push my finger down on one of my nostrils and suck in with the other nostril. Zap, bang, pow, the white powder disappears.

Two seconds later it's all gone and *I'mmmm* back. He's staring at me with a resounding nothing to say. 'What? Is there something on my face? What? What are you staring at? What is it?'

'Nothing, calm down.' He looks down the stairs and I know he's just trying to think of something to say before he can leave.

'What is it? What are you looking at? What?' It's like a one night stand without the sex.

'Well. If you see my dad, please tell him I'm upstairs. Ohh and thank you so much for the blow.'

Peter sees an out and he's down the stairs before I've wiped my nose. 'Bye.' He passes Brett, who's on his way up. Brett sits down next to me and touches my hair.

'Don't.'

'Do you want to drive me home?'

'No, well I'll drive you home if you remember where I parked the car. Brett where did I park the car?'

'That was a few days ago. You must have moved the car since then.'

I smile. 'Would you believe no?'

'Yes I would. I would believe Miranda Woke parked her car and can't find it.'

I exhale a gust of smoke all over. 'My dad's here.'

Brett frowns at first mention of my father. There are a few reasons Brett hates my father, topping the list is my father's comment to him about Eggs Benedict and cholesterol but that's another story. 'Really? I haven't seen him.'

'Well, he's here. He's supposedly in the VIP room.'

'Yeah?'

'That's what Laura said.'

'Laura's really cute.'

'Well she's married, so I wouldn't worry about it too much.'

'I give up.'

'I would hope. Listen I've got to find my dad. Please help me find him.'

Brett then proceeds to lodge his foot directly in his mouth. 'I saw that picture of your father in the *Observer*. I didn't think you had a little sister.'

'I don't. New wife.'

'Ohh.' He cracks his knuckles, trying to recover. 'So what's the plan?'

'Why do people ask me that? Do I seem like a person who could make and then keep plans?'

'No you don't.'

Mistyマ

We walk down the steps, through the room, around the grey-haired men to find my father. I inspect the ridges on each face. It feels like everyone's looking at me looking at them. I catch a grey-haired man's eye, him my last hope and me, his last chance at the power in being young, wrinkleless, smooth. Everyone wants to be young forever, or for a few more years and here I am, wasting it away. Someone once told me that if nothing else, I'd never be young again and that should be worth something, but it isn't, not to me anyway.

A blank-faced publicist guards the VIP room like it's filled with secret nuclear warheads. She's publicist-pretty: blonde hair tied flat with a hair dryer, white eye shadow carefully concealing the circles from her most recent drunken evening with some mogul in training and small black clothing hugging her flat butt which is fresh from Pilates class. She looks us up and down.

'Is Jason Woke in there?'

'And your name is?' She's right, I don't have the nicest outfit on, black dress, a little make-up smudge on the front, hair tied back in black ribbon. I could at least have blow-dried my hair or put on a little mascara or something.

'I think you know who I am.'

'Are you on the list?'

'Excuse me. Don't you know who I am?'

'Are you on the list?'

'I'm Miranda Woke. Jason Woke's daughter.'

'You're not on the list.'

'Excuse me, I'm Jason Woke's daughter.'

'Is that no?' I look up at Brett. He doesn't say anything.

'Yes, I mean no.' 'Why are you even here if you're not on the list?'

'I just want to get in to see my dad. He told me to meet him here.'

'Well. Wait here and I'll have someone go look.' A tall yellow man with elongated fingers and a slightly sheepish grin follows the point of her silk tip into the cafeteria.

He returns shaking his head.

'I'm sorry but Jason Woke supposedly left an hour ago.'

'What?'

'Kathy Gee said she saw him leave about thirty minutes ago.'

'Oh.'

'But.' She sounds cheerful; maybe this will be OK after all. 'But you, Miranda, actually are his daughter.'

'You think?'

'That's what Kathy Gee said.'

'Who?'

'You're still not on the list but I'll let you in.'

'Forget it.'

I'm high as a fucking kite, sharing air space with uber-asshole Peter Dean, trying to figure out how to get home, but an empty apartment filled with little cocaine mirrors and smoked cigarette butts seems like an anti-climactic ending to all this.

'We want to get back into the city. There are loads of other parties.' Peter speaks directly to a matte-Jersey girl, one of many in New York. The idea that there are more parties going on in this city fills me with dread.

'OK,' I say. Both of them turn to look at me.

'Well, maybe Will has a car,' Dean says, adjusting his tie so he looks comfortably ruffled, like a Brooks Brothers' warrior prince.

'Maybe. What's your girlfriend looking at?'

Nobody responds; they're moving through the parking lot toward the car.

'Fuck this.' I'm talking to myself now. 'No one returns my phone calls and there's no one who understands, and I'm all alone . . .'

I step carefully around a hunched-over grey-haired man sitting on the steps, notice his smell, a sort of musky old library smell. Some change drops out of my pocket and it makes a sound like a cracking china plate. I turn to pick up the quarters. Why waste a dollar? I scoop the change into my cupped right hand.

His voice is strangely familiar. 'Miranda Woke.'

'Huh?' Will's brown Chevy roars on the other side of the empty lot. The Chevy makes sounds like a hungry dog; it's filled with people and the windows are fogged.

'Miranda Woke.'

It's an honest mistake, calling the derelict dad.
'Dad?'

He looks at me, like he's going to say he loves
me, like he's going to say he's my dad, and that
he's been missing me. Don't I know he wants to
take me home?

'Don't you remember me?' And if he were my
dad, I'd tell him, I need him and forgive him. I just
want another chance.

'No,' I say to him, looking at the brown bag in
his hands, making out the silhouette of the bottle
through the bag.

'We met three summers ago in Rome.'

I scrunch my eyes up real tight, and try to
remember three summers ago, but come up blank.
I observe pieces of dandruff in his mustache.
Looking closer, I can see he's wearing good shoes,
the kind that are made in Italy and sell for four
hundred dollars. They are worn, but no more so
than my shoes.

'Right.'

He offers me the bag.

I deplete homeless man's supply of Wild Turkey,
accepting his offer with a wobbly hand. Wild
Turkey burns like vanilla extract, which I've also
had the pleasure of drinking. Gagging, I hand it
back to him. 'Thanks.' He looks at me, then at the
bottle. He hands the bottle back to me.

'Knock yourself out. There isn't much left
in there anyway and from the looks of you.
Well . . .' He holds the bottle up. I tilt the bottle

back and feel the contents slip down my throat, this time the Wild Turkey goes down like water.

I thank him.

I look at him, thinking he's going to ask me if I'm OK, but he just takes back the empty bottle of Wild Turkey, and tells me I'm in his sun.

What sun?

chapter six

'Ohh, shit,' I try.

'OHHH, SHIT. OHH, SHIT,' I try again.

'Ohh, my God. Ohh, my God. Brett. Brett.' My eyes won't open.

'Stop screaming, the bad part's over. You're awake. I wasn't sure you would.' Brett puts a warm wet wash cloth to my eyes. He dislodges the gunk and I'm free, no longer Helen Keller.

I scream when I see that Brett's white sheets are covered with big brown splotches of dried blood. The splotches look like inkblot tests. At first I think it's because I've gotten my period, but I quickly realize the ink bunnies are because my legs are bleeding or maybe it's my feet that are bleeding. A sharp pain is coming from my feet; I pull one of them up to my face for inspection. The foot itself is covered with dirt, blood, and bruises. Each bruise has its particular throb. I feel like my body is in pieces, like a giant jigsaw puzzle.

'So, Rip Vanna Winkle what's going on?' He leans over, brushing my skin with the black hairs on his arms. I feel him against me, his breathing heavy on my skin. There is a burning sensation all through my body, an aching but it's not for him, it's for some Valium. 'You've scared me before, but this time I thought I'd lost you.'

I turn on to my side, every single one of my ribs throbs. 'Yeah.' I cough. 'Yeah, why is that?' I have to push the words out.

'Don't you remember anything?'

'I remember PS1 and trying to find my father. And I remember coming up here, up all these steps and having the best sex with you. And wasn't I drinking Wild Turkey?'

'Ah, no. Best sex, any sex, I wish.'

'Well, what happened? Did I kill anyone?'

'No, you didn't kill anyone. Not funny. But beyond the usual Miranda Woke OD, you got yourself in a hell of a lot of real trouble. I'm not entirely sure what happened. I found you at four a.m. on the corner of Prince and Sullivan with no wallet, bleeding feet, screaming. I wouldn't have found you at all, but Weasome passed you on his way home from Double Happiness. He saved your life.'

'What life? How is Weasome? I haven't seen him in ages.'

'I don't know. All I know is that I'm taking you to your mother's house.'

'Sure, but she's not home.'

'No, she's home.'

'I think I know where my mother is. She's in

Paris at the Crillon. She's probably having some plastic surgery or an affair or something. And I hardly think this merits disturbing her vacation.'

'Her vacation has already been disturbed.'

'I don't want to know what you did.' I stop, breathe, wheeze, cough, drag in on a cigarette. 'I OD'd for a few hours and you call Godzilla. I can't leave you alone for a minute.'

'She's home, waiting to see you.'

'Whaaaattt?'

'I called her.'

'How dare you?'

'Listen, Miranda. You have no clue. Hello — clue phone, oh look it's for you.' His face is rippled with small delicate worry lines. 'She's not going to be mad, she wants to help you. She's been waiting for you to ask for help all along.'

'I think she's been waiting for a safer form of Botox all along, not for her daughter to come and tell her she's fucked it all up again. I'm thirsty. Where's the Wild Turkey?'

'You finished it.'

'So shoot me, OK? How about some vodka then?'

'We're not going to talk about anything and you're not going to drink anything else until we get to your mom's house. The car will be here soon. I can't deal with this now.'

'Fine.' I pull the grey blanket over my head and say, 'I think I'm dead. Thank God I'm still drunk, otherwise my body would really hurt.'

'You make it so hard, Miranda. Why do you have to make it so hard to like you?'

Do people not like me? 'I hardly think I'm the unlikable one.' I feel like I'm going to throw up, but I hold back; if my feet hurt now, imagine how they'll feel with all that weight on them. 'You, you have more issues than *Harper's Bazaar*. I'm nicer than a lot of people we know. My God, everything you say in therapy isn't necessarily grist for breakfast conversation. Get an editor. My God.'

'Whatever. At least I go to therapy. Odd, the people who need it don't seem to go.'

'A, I go; B, I don't necessarily need therapy; and C, I'm fine and you're the one with the drama problem.'

My answer is met with hysterical laughter.

I sit up and lean over the cheap wooden table and take a sip of Brett's bitter coffee. The coffee washes over my teeth. I can feel them coated with that strange cigarettey morning murk, like thin phlegm on each tooth.

'Let me make you some breakfast.'

He turns to the cabinet, where Bisquick lurks with the promise of salty pancakes, scones like dense pebbles, and vile biscuits with a baking soda aftertaste. With his back to me, I slide my hand into my little pony handbag and scoop out my emergency vial of blow, knock some on my palm and snort, snort, snort, snort. Brett turns around. He is furious. I look up from the last line, my nose burns, burns, burns.

'I can't believe it.'

'Can't believe what?'

'You almost died last night and now you're snorting cocaine this morning. You never used to be this bad.' Sometimes, often as I think about it, facts are just that, unsaid thoughts, and pieces of what really happened.

'What? Me? Bad? Define bad.'

'Fuck, Miranda. I think you're in a lot of trouble.'

'Stop being so fucking cryptic.' I put my nose down to the mirror and suck back a few more lines. Then I lean back on the brick wall, pick up my cigarette and relight.

'We'll talk about all this at your mom's. I can't deal with it now.' He speaks in exaggerated whispers, so low he sounds like a superagent whispering mink into the ear of his plumiest client at an Oscar party.

'Yeah, you mentioned that. I need a Valium. Where the fuck do you keep the Valium?'

'That's it!' He grabs my arm. 'Look at you.'

What drug addict isn't going to be filled with shame at a direction like that? He pulls a large hand mirror off the dresser. He shoves it in my face. 'Look.'

I open my eyes a little wider; it's the first time they are fully open. And when I look at her, I wonder who she is. She isn't a killer. She isn't a princess. And she used to have a chance, but now she doesn't any more.

*

The coke is wearing off and the wild hangover from the Wild Turkey is beginning to set in. If I weren't vomiting every ten minutes, I'd be terrified by the prospect of this little talk with my mother. But luckily all I can do is brace myself for the next wave of nausea.

Brett carries me up the narrow white limestone steps to the paneled cherry-wood door on Sixty-fourth Street. We stop. He looks at me and takes some of my hair in his hand.

'I want you to know, you're going to be OK.'

We have one of those long silences like you see in the movies but never believe normal people have. Romantic, sickening, confusing, and mildly annoying. He kisses me on the cheek.

I push him away and slam my hand on the doorbell.

Unfortunately the white façade of my mother's house is crumbling, otherwise it would be a beautiful house. It is one of those super-wide townhouses, the kind of house that is three windows across instead of two. I can hear a family of pigeons cooing from the space between the window and the air conditioner. The brown paint on the door is chipping. I remember when it wasn't.

The fashionable neurotic is looking at her square gold Cartier tank watch. She is pacing back and forth and she turns as we enter. Wisps of her brown hair peek out from under the hood of her grey cashmere sweat suit. She looks like she's going to jump on me as she races towards us.

'Miranda!' She wraps her arms around me. She used to smoke a hundred cigarettes a day; consequently her breath is still heavy, though she hasn't had a cigarette in a long time. Her eyes are puffy; she isn't wearing any make-up. I feel dizzy and lie down on the pink and yellow floral chiffon sofa. I do my best to ignore her by focussing on the ceiling's gold molding. Feeling my chest rise and fall is calming, quieting. My mouth is dry, but I'm too tired to ask for a nice little Stoli gimlet.

'Does anyone want a little drink? You look tense, Brett. Can I offer you a Scotch?' She gets up and walks to the bar. My mother the socialite, born into a long line of new money. Her father was a famous alcoholic, who also directed movies. Her mother was a famous alcoholic, who also acted. They both drank famously and performed mediocrely. Both died before sixty.

'No. I think I'm fine, and Miranda's more than covered in that department.'

She puts some lime in her Diet Coke. 'So, darlings . . .'

'Look at her.' Brett points to the couch and I guess to me, but I feel invisible.

'Well, darlings . . .' She takes a sip. Mom's the kind of woman who can't stand, sit, or lay still for even a minute. She glides, Diet Coke in hand, around the room. Little drops of water have formed on the side of her glass. They slide off onto the rug, like the living room is a tiny ecosystem and her glass is a rain cloud.

She putters, adjusting the vase on the mantle, moving some pictures around, descending back into them, into her old life with my father in Paris. She's trying to find some order in the silver frames and in the old sepia pictures of other people's immigrant relatives.

'Are you two on or off right now?'

'Off, and we've been that way for a year,' I say with zeal. As soon as I do I regret it, because Brett looks unbelievably hurt.

I can see it in her face, the change as she remembers that I have told her this. Her expression shifts to a smile. 'Oh my God. I'm sorry. I'm just the tiniest bit off today.' I giggle; she's the tiniest bit off every day. 'I don't know what's upset me so much,' she says, looking at my hands that are shaking. Maybe I have an early onset of Parkinson's. She laughs in a nervous contained way and taps her Belgian loafers on the rug.

'Maybe we should go talk about this somewhere.' Brett motions to Mom.

She turns, abruptly and angularly, like a Chihuahua on crack. 'Brett, why don't we go into the kitchen?'

Brett looks at Mom. Mom looks at her drink. I look for a cigarette. I find a cigarette and light it. Mom says something about me not being allowed to smoke in the house. Some of the ash falls on the couch. Mom runs to get an ashtray. Poody, the twenty-nine-year-old poodle who is blind and deaf, walks into the room and shits on the carpet.

Believe me, there's a reason why I drink and I'm in the midst of it.

'Darling, we're going into the kitchen. You just rest there. Alright?' She arranges a yellow blanket over my feet before leaving the room. I lean back; the nausea is again having its way with me. I can hear their slightly muted voices, but I really don't care enough to perform a full eavesdrop.

From the moment Jeff died till right now, everything has seemed like a short Claymation sketch, with singing raisins advertising candy.

'This isn't what I need. I'm horribly busy. I've got to give it to her, she has absolutely the worst timing.' She's screaming, like I've crossed the invisible line of what is annoying and what is the kind of thing that'd get me disinherited.

'But, Diana, don't you see, she's losing.'

I close my eyes, trying as hard as I can to catch each word in the drums of my ears, but they keep coming out. His voice gets lost in the noise of the kitchen appliances.

'All we have to do is book a flight.'

A flight? A flight to where? I hope this isn't another one of my mother's duty-free missions.

I start to fade. I need a drink. Why has no one offered me a drink? I pull myself up and wobble to the two-story mirrored bar, with the intention of pouring myself a drink, the expensive stuff; but the thin frosted bottles with pictures of trees etched into them are on the top shelf, just out of reach. The plastic quart of Popernoff sits just below my hand on the mirrored counter top. I grab it, mix it in a big yellow glass tumbler with orange juice so it doesn't look like vodka. I finish the drink before I get back to the sofa. For a rich person, my mother is awfully cheap about her boozes – pushing the Popernoff, how rude. I lie back down on the sofa, better.

I close my eyes and drift.

'Miranda,' Brett calls, as he walks slowly through the peach-colored doorway and sits down next to me. 'Your mom's going to take you to the airport.'

'What? How long have I been asleep?' I breathe in and take a piece of candy off the coffee table.

'About two hours.'

'I feel better. A little sleep and *voilà*, I'm fine.'

'You are not fine. Your mother's taking you to the airport; you'll be on the two a.m. flight.'

'Two a.m. Who the fuck takes a fucking two a.m. plane?' I unwrap the piece of candy, playing with the wrapper so it makes a very annoying sound.

'You.'

'OWWWW!' I grab my stomach and put my hand on my mouth. Brett runs to put a yellow garbage can in front of me. Just in time: barely miss vomiting all over the sofa. My skin feels like it's covered with red ants.

When I finish, I glance up at Brett. 'Sorry.'

'It's fine.'

I feel that really great high you get after vomiting, like everything in the world is right.

'Ohhh, my God, Miranda!' Mom rushes into the room late as usual.

'I'm fine. Just a bit hot.' But from the way Brett and Mom look at me I can tell I'm blatantly not fine.

Brett helps me lie down on the sofa, but I'm so hot and sore that I can't find a comfortable position.

I hear my mother on the phone to the doctor. I see the yellow molding staring down at me.

'Doctor Winksteanberge says you can take some Valium. They'll calm you down and they'll also prevent you from having a seizure. I know you like Valium.' She laughs.

Now, that's the understatement of the year. Mom hands me the bottle with the little orange label.

Brett hands me a glass of water. Mom goes upstairs to get a jacket and a handbag. I swallow a handful of white pills and feel better instantly. The room isn't as hot and the floor isn't spinning quite as fast; even my arms don't feel as sore.

'What happened to me?'

'You just self-destructed.'

'That's not what I meant.'

'I'm not entirely sure what happened to you last night, if that's what you're asking me. All I know is, you must have made it back through the Midtown Tunnel in Will's brown Chevy, but they told me that you insisted they let you off in alphabet city, I'm not entirely sure why. And I know you took some blow from Janice's bag when you got out of the car. It would have been the usual Miranda lost weekend, except you've never ended up half dead before.

'Weasome called me from his cell phone. He said you were screaming curses at the garbage bags on the street. I came as fast as I could but I wasn't ready for what you looked like. The whites of your eyes were completely red. There was something that came out of your mouth, a kind of white paste thing. Your feet were bleeding; you were screaming; and there was something very strange about the way you were walking. I don't know, Rand . . . it was really awful, really awful. I've seen you bad, but this . . . this was beyond anything I've ever seen.

'I asked you what you took and you wouldn't tell me. I asked you what the matter was and you said you couldn't find your dad. I begged you to tell me what you needed and you told me you wanted a quiet place to die. Weasome and I took you to my apartment in a taxi. You kept screaming about things not working and after hours and heroin. When I got you home, your condition was much, much worse.'

I look up at him.

'Then I put compresses on your head, but you were so hot, there was nothing to do with you. Nothing at all. Then, well . . .' He stops and takes a sip of water. I can see he's upset, flustered. 'You were dying, so I had to get Weasome to . . .'

'I think I get the idea.' I feel so small.

'No, Randa. Listen.'

'What?'

'For a minute, or two, or something, you stopped breathing. Luckily Weasome knew CPR, otherwise you'd be dead right now.'

'Stop.'

'No, he did CPR, and then well, we got you back but . . .'

'I get it.'

'No. No, you don't.'

'You're torturing me.'

'Randa. Listen to me. Listen to me, look at me. I've been through so much with you.'

'Fine. I'm sorry.'

'NO. Listen to what happened.'

'I said I'm sorry.'

'No. Listen to me.'

chapter seven

We have tons of stuff. We're a stuff kind of family, a ten-suitcase, five-pound-handbag, three-shopping-cart kind of family. When Mom comes down the stairs she is laden with stuff: her jacket, her handbag, her cell phone, her makeup kit, her scarf, her hat, her dog, her maid, her purse-size decanter of Valium, and I'm sure I'm forgetting something. She's holding the cordless house phone in one hand and Poody in the other. She looks like she hasn't stopped moving in three days. She stops at the foot of the stairs. She drops the phone, the dog, and all her stuff on the floor.

'All right, Miranda. I'm going to drive you to the airport.'

'You are night-blind.'

'How about if we call you two a car, how does that sound?' Brett says, chewing some sugarless gum he bought on the way here.

'You'll get to Minnesota at five. They'll pick you up at the airport. You have a ticket on United Airlines flight seven forty-one' Mom recites the itinerary. I close my eyes and look at my life, where everything that could went wrong.

I lie back on the pink-and-yellow floral sofa, an alarming mix of country and classical. I start to drift back into sleep. Brett's good-bye rings in my ears. But I never got to say a real good-bye, which is the story of my life.

Eventually Mom wakes me and we get into the car. The driver talks too much, tells us the history of the city, describing each building in painful detail, as we roll our eyes at each other and the car weaves in and out of traffic. Honking and yelling follow us everywhere.

It's raining. Soft, large wet drops fall on the windshield, blend into each other, become part of the glass. I'm not drunk, and every building, taxi, parked car I see is sobering, sickening. Even the windshield provokes nausea

'I'm concerned, Randa.'

'Why? 'Cause I almost OD'd and died last night, or is there another reason?'

'No, that's why.' She sits back in her seat, settled in her gray cashmere shawl, behind her little square glasses that make her look like she has a job. She holds a little brown paper bag full of candy. She shoves candy corns into her mouth like it's the Last Supper.

'I don't know what to say. I'm sorry?'

'Don't be sorry, darling. That's not what this is about.'

'What is it about then?' I chew another Valium

in hopes it'll make the aching in my bone marrow stop.

I turn back to her. Her little glasses are fogged up, she is crying. The driver turns around to offer a soggy Kleenex. Mom waves her hand at him, banishing him back to the steering wheel. The traffic isn't moving. I hope we miss the plane.

'This . . .' She gathers her thoughts, but into what is a mystery. 'This is about me failing you.' She breathes in. 'I've failed you. I've failed you.' She cries, mostly for her own benefit. 'I understand I've let you down, but I'm just so glad that you've come back. And now I can help you.' She wipes her little nose on the sleeve of her gray sweater.

'Oh, I think you'll find time to get back to Paris.' I realize I never listen to her. Actually we don't listen to each other, and consequently our conversations turn into dueling internal monologues. The traffic is moving again. I look at the blue face of my watch and pick a candy corn out of the brown paper bag. I put it in my mouth and feel the sugar eat away at the enamel on my teeth.

'Miranda, I'm offering my help to you.'

'I don't know why. This has nothing to do with you. This isn't about the fact that you missed my seventh birthday or how my father got remarried, or why you and my father got divorced, or how you just got your chin done. This is about me and that's it. Me and my drugs.'

'Fine. I understand.'

Her completely cool response just feeds my rage. 'No, you don't.'

She looks down at my shaking right hand.

'Sweetie. This is all going to be okay.' She sighs. 'Everything is going to be okay.'

'How do you know?'

The inside of the car is warm and dark, the little light behind her head is on, and all the ridges in her face make shadows on her tight skin. 'I just know.' She touches me like I'm some kind of anonymous hospital patient wounded by a land mine, one that her charity raises money for.

'Mom, I honestly don't know what's going to happen to me.' I can feel the distance in the way her hands move on my arm, and it makes me scared. I don't want to do anything that's going to make her stop loving me. 'I want to get better.'

'Things will work out.' I can feel she doesn't recognize me anymore, doesn't remember when I was cute and small and didn't do this kind of thing. When I wasn't bouncing in and out of therapists' offices, when I was like anyone else, normal, safe, regular.

'Promise?'

The car skids to a halt in front of the terminal. A friendly skycap takes my bags and smiles at me; he has a gleam of blue in his dark brown eyes. I wonder if he has ever seen a rehab good-bye before.

Mom doesn't talk to me. In a move that seems out of character for her, she walks over to the trunk and helps with the black duffel. She lowers her eyes so that all she can see is the trunk. I try to catch her eye, but she just looks at the silent skycap throwing my bags on the trolley.

'So.' Mom's pain is in her eyes, in the sagging of her lips, in the places she looks old and in the places where the skin is so tight it has no place to go. As we face each other, her on one side of the car, me on the other, I can almost feel her cashmere arms around me.

'So.' I have to remember that this is happening to me. This all feels like some fantastic story, some movie seen on seventies celluloid.

'The ticket's at the counter under your name.'

'I know.'

'All you need to do is show your driver's license.'

'Okay.'

'Can you do that?'

'I'm a drug addict, not an idiot.'

'Are your hands still shaking?'

'Not as much,' I lie.

'I love you.'

'I know.'

'Call me when you get there.'

'I will.'

'Don't worry, planes can fly in rain. Just because it's raining doesn't mean it's dangerous.'

'Mom, thanks for the ride.'

'Darling?'

'Yes?'

• Molly Jong-Fast

'I love you very much. You know that, don't you?'

At 1:00 A.M. the first-class lounge is almost empty. It's deceiving to call it the first-class lounge because the immediate connotation is a clean, well-lighted space, filled with attractive rich people sipping beautiful tropical drinks. But this is domestic.

The domestic first-class lounge is dark, filled with smoked mirrors and old green glass ashtrays advertising varieties of beer that haven't been available for years. It's decorated with bowls of salty hepatitis peanuts and pretzels. The room reeks of a fight between mildew and air freshener. The mildew is winning. There are a few lone businessmen drinking and watching sports on the TV that hangs off a wire over the bar.

Everyone turns to check out nineteen-year-old me, hardly able to breathe in tight leather clam diggers, complemented by a white pony-skin tank top and a sheer pink cashmere poncho. On my feet are a pair of Manolos, decorated with a crystal mosaic of the New York skyline. A giant Hermes bag in lime-green leather with bronze fixtures is my only carry-on.

'Three vodka cranberries.'

The waitress looks at me.

'Three vodka cranberries.'

The overworked waitress forces a smile; she pushes her bleached blond hair behind her ears. It

• 128

occurs to me, while folding my drink napkin into a sailor's hat, that it might be humiliating to have a nineteen-year-old with rhinestone shoes barking orders at you a 1:00 A.M. She lays the drinks next to each other. Airport bars make the best drinks – strong, cheap (the lounge bar is free), and to the point. The vodka swirls like gasoline in my glass.

I pull out my brown paper bag, fill my mouth with candy corn and start to chew.

I order two more drinks.

Finally, the loudspeaker announces my flight. Thunder bangs on the roof like it's trying to get in, but I'd be hard pressed to think of why anything would want to get in here.

I start on my fourth drink. The announcement is made again. The bar stool is covered in this fake brown leather. I slide off it and regain my balance when I am almost on the floor.

The businessmen turn to ignore me.

Dragging my carry-on behind me, I get on the moving walkway and, like a blip on a radar screen, grow smaller and smaller.

The most important person in first class always gets seat l-A: the usual movie star, model, or mogul. For the 2:00 A.M. flight to Minnesota, which I think they should rename the rehab shuttle, I am sitting in l-A – from which we can deduce there is no one else in first class. The stewardess walks over to me.

'Welcome. May I get you something to drink?'

From her voice it's clear she's been born more than once.

'Vodka, straight up.' I don't look at her. I keep my eyes ahead. I knock a few Valium out of the bottle.

'You're a little young to be drinking.' It occurs to me that she might be right. If only someone had mentioned this a little sooner.

'Oh, my God, you're right. I am too young to be drinking. What was I thinking? What could I have possibly been thinking?' I lean back in my seat. I push a shaking hand in her face. 'I wonder if I'm too young to have DTs.' She looks at me, then at the drink cart. She fixes me the drink and puts it down in front of me.

'I'll just keep bringing you drinks.' She smiles, arranging a package of peanuts next to me.

'Fine.'

Someone once said, 'There are no atheists on airplanes.' I grip the armrest as the plane wobbles to regain its balance. For a slip of a second I feel how thin this life really is, how I could fall into the other side by accident, without ever having a choice.

The stewardess arrives with another drink, and I suck it back. The compressed airplane air hits my face. 'We're experiencing some bad weather. Please keep your seat belts fastened.' The pilot announces.

Veins pop out of my old hands like electrical wires. My hands red like Jeff's.

When I think about it now, I know I wanted him, in the way obsession takes its victims regardless of who they are or how little they are capable of. I remember brushing his teeth after an eight-day spree. But even at my weakest, my most susceptible, I knew obsession and love were not the same thing. I knew we were just a pantomime of the real thing, genuine fakes. But I still miss him.

The paper-covered pillow falls from my back and I finish what's left of my drink, my last drink: cheap vodka (Popernoff) and flat tonic water. I close my eyes.

We hit the ground with the first of many bumps.

From the look of Daisy, it's obvious she's a reformed northerner born bastard daughter of hippie parents who were tripping when they named her. Daisy is the typical Minne-sober transplant. She got sober here and never left, and now she's got frosty blond hair and pink eye shadow spread thinly on her eyelids. Her nails match her outfit and her pack of gum. When she opens her mouth she speaks every cliché of a shampoo commercial, as if sobriety meant stupidity and good hair.

She looks cautiously at me. She can't actually say she's from Hazelden; it's a kind of secret code that they have to observe. Anonymity or something.

'Miranda?'

'Yeah?'

'I'm Daisy,' she says between chews. The airport is small and so cold that you can see your breath freeze. I stand in front of carousel 3, looking at her feet.

'Good. I'm so tired.'

'Well, that's normal.'

'Will you help me with my bags?'

'That's why I'm here. They should be coming down that ramp.'

'Thanks.' I smile at her.

We grab the bags and head for the car.

'Okay,' she twangs, as she gets into the driver's seat. I glance up at her eyes. Eye contact is important because it makes people think they can trust you.

Grinning at me, she turns on some hokey country station and pulls the large station wagon out of the lot onto the icy two-lane highway.

'So, um, how long is the drive?' I look with dismay at the speedometer, she's pushing thirty.

'Two hours.'

'Great. So . . .'

'Try to sleep.'

'Oh, okay.' We drive through St. Paul, past quaint little houses where normal people live. We drive past schools; in a few hours those schools will be filled with normal children. We drive down icy roads, past frozen lakes and ice. It occurs to me, in the face of all this that I am definitely not normal.

I play with the electric windows, looking at Daisy to see if this is going to annoy her.

'Would you mind . . .'

'What?'

'Would you mind not doing that?'

'This?' I move the window up and down.

'Yeah. That's it.'

'What?'

'Why don' t you try and rest.'

'Fine.' I relinquish control of the window.

Maybe I'm unconscious, dreaming, whatever. I press my face against the cold glass, like I might have when I was little.

Somewhere along the way, in one those towns in northern Minnesota spelled with at least one umlaut, I hold my left hand up into the light. There is nothing delicate about my hands, hands that don't even look like they belong to a girl. A big blue vein pops through my skin, which is pasty, like Elmer's glue. I twist my right hand into a ball. A little bit of sun shines on the cuts, bruises, burns, and bite marks that mar the skin. I hold my hand to the window and realize the sun is almost up.

chapter eight

There is only one way to come to rehab: drunk, so drunk that you can't walk. I guess I got that part right.

We arrive. Now it's me and the rehab door and thousands of acres of arctic Minnesota tundra. Daisy drives away in the stationwagon off to pick up the next model, movie star or mogal.

I look at the horseshoe of modern, light-red brick buildings, institutional architecture that reminds me of prisons or college dorms. Each building engages the other in a dialogue, each angle telling a story to the other.

There may be something meaningful to say about rehabs, about the culture of them, about the kind of people who spend their whole lives in and out of them, but I couldn't tell you what that is.

The door slams behind me, making a mechanical locking sound that seems like an atom-bomb explosion. Life is over.

I push through the door, trip on the lintel; at least I've made an entrance.

An obese nurse meets me. We are alone in the nurses' station surrounded by carpeted hallway. The nurses' station consists of a bunch of white countertops, behind which are locked boxes filled with enough meds to rival my medicine cabinet at home. She tells me to take a seat in a brown plastic chair lodged between a pay phone and a soda machine. The detox Mother Mary's (Hall (M&M for short) is a cross between a hospital and a motel: oxygen tanks and little paper-wrapped soaps.

She takes my shoelaces, pulls them right out of the little rings in my sneakers. 'Just in case,' she says, sliding her hands around the folded sweaters in my suitcase, careful not to unfold anything more than necessary, taking my bottle of Chanel Allure, my nail-polish remover, and my green toner.

'Hey.'

'Just in case.'

'Just in case I smell good, have clear skin and polished nails – wouldn't want that, would we?'

She points to the labels, schoolmarmishly. 'These have alcohol in them. Don't want you drinking any of these.'

'Listen, I'm exhausted.'

'Fine,' she says. 'I just have some forms for you. You need to sign them before you go to bed.' She hands me a stack of papers that make the Watergate files look like *Goodnight Moon*.

I sprawl my signature all over everything. 'Here. Now I need a bed. I like linen sheets, and some large bath towels.

'You're in room number five,' she points. 'Everything you'll need is in there.'

'You have a gym, right?' I smile. 'Muscle tone is the first to go.'

Detoxing hurts. Here are few of the highlights: – vomiting, sweating, shaking, headache, sore throat, and diarrhoea.

'How long, Miranda Woke? How long has it been?' Julia pushes open the door just a crack and the room fills with fluorescent light from the hallway. Her shadow follows her across the green carpet.

'Julia, what are you doing here?' Okay, stupid question but what else is there to say? I look at her. A Rubenesque freckled moon of a face is framed by dirty, stringy hair. Julia, the woman who used to be perfectly done for every occasion, has unwashed hair.

'Hey, sleeping beauty. Sorry to wake you, but it's been a week.' She smiles at me. She looks remarkably unperfect, nice, kind of fat.

'What? A week? It doesn't feel like a week. It feels more like seven days.' Where's my half grapefruit and fresh-squeezed orange juice? Where are the mints on my pillow?

'Don't worry.' She smiles. 'The worst is over. The detox is just remnants, it just passed in flux, baby.

I am not going to ask you how you got here. I
know how.' She laughs.

'How long have you been here?' The two-
dimensional quality of the starkly furnished room
makes me feel like I'm in a Pet Shop Boys video.
Everything is flat, flat, flat.

'Oh, I'm going back to the city, EL CITY in two
days. They wanted me to go to a halfway house,
but I said . . . I said . . .' A somewhat despon-
dent nurse walks by the open door. She is wearing
a matching floral shirt and pleated pants; I notice
that polyester floral prints are not slimming. She
pauses in the doorway, looks at me, and sticks her
finger up like a small bratwurst. She mouths,
'You've got one minute.'

'. . . I said, "Whoa, man, I used to be a model,"
– okay it was like for five minutes in Japan, but
still, I mean, I've written for *Tatler*, hell, I've been
a fucking feature in *Tatler*. I hardly consider myself
a candidate for a halfway house. Do you?'

'No.'

'Whatever, whatever. Don't worry, Randa,
you're supposed to be nuts. You've only been
sober for, like, not even a day. Anyway, the only
halfway house I'm going to is the Four fucking
Seasons.' Julia ignores the nurse and continues
talking to me. 'But, whatever, none of that outside
bullshit means anything in here.' She giggles.
'You'll see, Randa. Try dropping a name. Try
getting sympathy for not being able to find a dry
cleaner.'

'But I thought famous people came here.'

'They do.'

'But no dry cleaning.' I say it like it's the worst news I've heard.

'And there's no tiping,' she pauses. 'You don't look so well,' Julia says leaning over me; her arms are covered with healing track marks.

'They've healed really well.' I point to the marks.

'Yeah.'

'Neosporin?'

'I don't know, but after the doctor cut the abscess out of my leg the nurses started applying something to my arms.'

'Abscess?' I sit up in my bed.

'Yeah.' She leans forward, like she's telling me a scary bedtime story.

'Shit, Julia.'

'It's not that bad. It was in my leg. I mean really, it's not like it was in my arm. When they're in your arm, that's bad. This isn't that bad. You know?'

'It's all bad. What happened?' I suck in a breath; it hurts when I talk. 'The last time I saw you, you were in Bill Blass dancing with the Famous Guy at MoMA.'

'Yeah. That was the worst. I don't think I've ever been more unhappy than I was at that moment.' She starts playing with the tongue on her red Pumas.

'When was the first time I met you, Miranda Woke?'

'God. I don't remember. But you were dating the Famous Guy.' Julia grimaces. 'How is the Famous Guy?'

'Didn't I meet you through Jeff?'

'Yeah, we must have met at that party he had. The one at his loft.'

'Did you know he died?'

'Yeah, I'm well aware. I was at the funeral.' I don't mention I killed him. That might just be a tad too personal for this conversation.

'Did you know he was sick?'

'Hepatitis. I spent a lot of time with him before he died.'

'Did you share needles with him? Because he fucked a lot of girls . . . and he was in shooting galleries in Harlem. I mean, he was really a dirty guy.'

'Don't say that.'

'What? I'm just saying Jeff never was the condom type. He used to fuck prostitutes. All the time. And he was bi, you know, girls and guys and farm animals. Did you know that?'

'No.'

'Well, I should know. I fucked him.'

'What?' I can feel the embarrassment wash over me. I hate her. Bitch. I feel sick. My heart runs through my chest.

'Well . . .'

'Well, what?'

'I should tell you because everybody already knows. I have AIDS. I don't think I got it from Jeff, but I very well might have. Hard to know, now that he's fucking offed himself. Typical to leave before any of us had a chance to find out. But I should have expected this from him. He said we were going to go away. He was going to take me somewhere, then, like, four days later he's dead. Typical, he was always so unreliable, irresponsible, such a fucking liar.'

'You mean HIV.'

'No.' She shakes her head. 'I mean what I mean and I mean AIDS.' I can hear her grinding her molars together. 'I' m dying.'

'Did you get a second opinion?'

'A second opinion on AIDS?'

'Well, a second test?'

'Trust me, who doesn't get a second opinion on death, or AIDS or whatever it is that's killing me right now.'

'Does the Famous Guy?'

'What?'

'Does he have it?'

'I can't say. Come on, Randa, you know the way this works. Things get out, get told to people, and before you know it, you're going from a blind mention on Page Six to a cover story in *New York* magazine. And you know what would happen with his wife? And with his kids? No, I'm not going to do any more damage than I already have. He's a very high-profile person. You know?'

'I know.' I feel stupid for saying anything about

the Famous Guy. 'But you're sick.' I pull the comforter around my neck.

'Not sick, dying.'

I was trying not to sleep, but I seem to have failed miserably. Because some big old doctor with a face like a mule is trying to wake me up. He has lines in his forehead that look like they're cast in papier-mâché, and jowls so loose they must flap in the wind when he walks. He leans too close to me – like I've lost the privilege of personal space.

'We're going to start an IV for you.' I can't understand the rest of what he says and am more than thrilled when he leaves the room. Unfortunately, he leaves the door open.

I hear him go away, his feet loud on the linoleum. A skinny strung-out white guy dressed only in sky-blue boxer shorts runs by my room, hysterical, screaming.

Dr Mule Face comes back in, doom resting around his lips where the five o'clock shadow should be. He thinks I can't tell, as he nods to a few nurses who come in to see what a destroyed nineteen-year-old looks like. I feel like one of those animals at the zoo.

A nurse who looks like a female version of Larry Flynt tries to take my blood pressure. She doesn't have much success with the armband; she gives up and leaves the room. Nurse Floral takes her place, sticking my hand with a small needle.

'You have bad veins,' she tells me, as she cuts off

all the circulation in my arm and my hand turns every shade of blue.

'Bad veins?'

'You have the worst veins I've ever seen. And you shoot heroin?' I fold my arm and point to the green vein that forms in the inside of my elbow.

'If only that were the worst thing about me,' I laugh.

Miss Larry Flynt asks me if I'd like some food. I tell her I would not like some food and I do not appreciate this clear conspiracy to make me fat. Fauna in flora polyester tells me she'll come back in fifteen minutes. I feel the saline solution drip into my veins. And all the nurses are gone to sicker patients.

I wake up, feeling almost gleeful. The tubes are gone. There's a Band-Aid and a bruise on my arm. Flora in fauna carries a clipboard. She looks good today. Maybe she went a little lighter on the foundation, maybe it's her nice silver earrings.

'So, Miranda. I think we're gonna need to get you moving. Come on, get up.'

'No.' I drop my head back on the pillow.

'Come on, honey. You've been in bed for eight days. We need to see what kind of condition you're in, and the way to do that is to get you walking.' She has what my grandmother would call regular features: a face like a clock, nose dead center, eyes placed at each corner of her square face.

'Fuck it. Fine.' I move to get up and fall out of the hospital bed, right through the metal arms made to prevent this very thing.

The nurse holds me until I can stand on my own.

'Okay. Now just walk to me.'

'Unlikely.' I laugh at her under my breath.

'Just walk over to me.'

'No.' I'm swaying, barely standing now.

'Defiance just makes us sicker.' What is she talking about? There is no 'us.' I see no 'us.' All I see is me in a paper dress that doesn't close that my ass hangs out of.

'I can't.' I say, grabbing the floral drape behind me.

She stands a long, dark ten feet from me. There is a doorway in between us. She smiles. 'Come on, just a few steps. I need to find out that you're okay.' She pleads with me as if I have a choice. Damage control is not akin to free will – hubris might make me think it is, but it's not. What's that smell. Is it me?

I take one step and find myself on the linoleum.

'Come on, dear. Let me help.' She reaches for my arm.

'No, don't fucking touch me.'

'Just let me help you get to your feet.'

'Don't touch me, you fat fuck.'

'Come on. Don't be discouraged.'

'FUCK YOU, YOU FAT PIECE OF SHIT. FUCK

YOU, WHITE TRAILER TRASH. DON'T FUCKING TOUCH ME. DON'T FUCKIN' TOUCH ME.'

'I don't take abuse. From anyone, ever.' She looks at me, turns, and walks away, leaving me alone in the middle of the room. Lying on my face. I smell like a horse in central park. Ugh.

'Help!' They've taken my watch so I have no place to look, but I think I've been lying on the floor for a long time. Time really doesn't matter here. The only visible difference between night and day is that night is when the nurses do the checks, to make sure you haven't strangled yourself with your bedsheets. Every fifteen to twenty minutes it's click, turn, click, slam. And day is when the bloated new patients arrive.

'Are you ready to give it one more try?' She appears hovering over me.

'I'm sorry.'

'Don't be.'

'I'm so sorry.' I start crying. I would run from me, if I could.

'It's okay. Don't worry, honey. I know what this is like. I was a heroin addict ten years go,' she says casually. 'Now I'm in recovery.' She lifts me back into the bed and pulls the blanket up to my chin. The blanket is covered with other people's vomit stains. She closes the door. I'm comforted by the knowledge she'll be back in fifteen to twenty minutes to make sure I haven't killed myself.

*

The nurses say you come back in this order: physically, mentally, and spiritually. Physically is what I'm working on now. I can thank three years of daily Valium use for my failing muscles and my lack of hand/eye coordination. Of course nineteen-year-olds get better fast, and I'm walking now. I can now walk almost the entire length of the detox. Which means the TV lounge is now part of my territory.

The TV lounge has brown couches, brown shades, brown carpeting, and vending machines that are also brown. A man I've deemed Cast Man, because of the cast on his arm, sits on the brown couch. He is as permanent a fixture on that couch as the brown shades are on the windows. I'm a new *Wheel* watcher, making up a strong part of the eighteen-to-twenty-four age group that watches the aging game show. I look at *Wheel of Fortune* and its host, the illustrious Pat Sajak. Pat smiles – clearly he has no problems; I on the other hand have nothing but.

While Vanna's turning letters and looking svelte in a beaded silver gown, I get my first rehab phone call. The pay phone is in the middle of the hallway, a place where all the other patients and nurses can hear your conversation, a place where it's difficult to discuss anything illicit.

'Hello.'

'Miranda?'

'Brett.' Not Mom.

'So, how ya doing?' Brett's voice competes with the traffic. He must be on his cell phone.

'Good, except for the fact that . . . there has been some kind of big mistake. I shouldn't be here. These people, Brett, these people are really sick. I'm not this sick. These people have some real problems, I mean really—'

'Nurse! Nurse! A tall, good-looking shirtless junkie screams at the nurse from outside the heavy glass doors. 'I need some meds! Come on, MEDS! THIS FUCKIN' PLACE SUCKS! I WANT KLONDEN PATCHES, AND I WANT THEM NOW!' He leans his head off the terrace and vomits what looks like at least four days' worth of fast food.

'MIRANDA.'

'Yeah, Brett, I'm here.'

'What's going on there?'

'Oh, just people flipping out. This is not a safe place for someone like me.'

'I wish I could help you. My shrink thinks enabling you is helping both of us stay sick.'

'You're so deeply full of shit. But you know what? It's fine. It's fuckin' fine. You know why, Fat Boy? Because I'll just get someone else to buy me a ticket.'

'You're fucking crazy. Though after spending some time with your mother, I completely understand why you're such a total lunatic.'

'Well, thank you for that little insight into my family. I hope you won't be terribly insulted if I hang up on you now. *Ciao*!' A nurse walks by and hushes me.

'Wait!'

'What?'

'I'll get you a ticket.'

'Yeah?' I don't really believe him but I'm willing to play along.

'Yeah. I want you home. I miss you.'

'Really?'

'I want you back here with me.'

'Brett, you're the best. I love you so much.'

'I just thought of something. If I get you a ticket now, then you can get to the Warhol party at the Whitney later on this week.'

My black party dress should be back from the cleaners, and I can wear my black Prada boots. Where are my black Prada boots? And then I stop myself, feel something tug on my arm, turn around to see nothing there.

'Listen, Brett, I gotta go.'

'Are you coming home?'

'No.'

The shirtless junkie screams for a nurse. He has now taken off all his clothing and is running around naked. Outside the leaves are blowing off the trees. Cast Man with yellow hair and eyes staggers past me. This is where I belong.

'So what are you saying?'

'I'm saying . . .' I have a huge lump in my throat.

'You're going to stay?

'Yes.' I start to cry. 'I killed Jeff.' It feels good to finally say it.

'Randa, I promise, swear to you. You didn't do anything wrong. You didn't kill Jeff.'

'Are you sure?'

'Yeah. You can't make someone choke to death on their own vomit, no matter how much you might want them to.' He stops.

'What do you mean? I didn't want him to die.'

'I love you.' I hear the question in that, hear him directing the taxi driver where to go, hear the taxi bump over the cobblestones in the streets of SoHo. 'But you already knew that. Didn't you?'

'Yeah, I knew.'

'Do you want to try again with me?'

'Brett, you have the worst timing. Can we talk about this later?' I look out the heavy glass doors. The naked junkie is talking to the Cast Man. The leaves blow around the two of them like halos.

'Miranda, can you just—'

'I gotta go, Brett. He is still talking when I hang up the phone. I hear my own breath on the receiver; it smells like disinfectant. The sound system booms my name, calling me for another evaluation. I want to move but I can't. I curl up in the chair next to the phone.

I've asked God to make a choice – to kill me or to save me. And I'm paralyzed by the answer.

chapter nine

Hazelford is not Harvard. I glance down at my white hospital slippers. I'm guessing the kids at Harvard are probably not wearing slippers, peeing in a cup in front of an over-inflated nurse, who is clad head-to-toe in floral flammable fabric.

Whitney flies through the door. Across her face is one of those large saccharine smiles I hate. Everything I have is crumpled back into two suitcases. Picking up one of the suitcases, Whitney is a hurricane of friendly instructions.

'Hey, Miranda, right?'

'Yeah.'

'. . . RRRRight. . . RRRRight? WWWell, I'm Whitney. Whitney Jane. But you can call me Whit. I'll be your buddy.'

'Lucky me.'

'I've come to take you down to the Rose Unit. The Rose Unit's nice, . . . you'll like it. Don't worry. Are you nervous? 'Cause there's no reason to be nervous. I've been here . . .' She stops to reflect on her own stream of constant chatter. I am trying to stuff one more sweater into my bag, which is beyond full with raincoats and evening gowns. I am trying not to listen to Whitney because just the sight of her gives me a splitting headache. 'I've been here twice.' She looks at me for a reaction.

'That's right, twice. And I'm only twenty-three. How old are you?' She speaks like a rich Texan, but looks like Stevie Nicks with her black sweat pants and long black tee shirt. Her body is uneven, her legs are much fatter than her arms, as if the weight she recently gained doesn't know where to go.

'Nineteen.' I pull my tight itchy grey wool Chanel sweater on over my head. It gives me a horrible rash of red dots across my chest. I know, I know, I know – I'm such a label whore. But there are labels and then there's quality and I'm willing to suffer for the finest wool North Ireland has to offer. After all, what's a little rash in the face of craftsmanship? In Judaism it's not how much money you have but how much money you spend that makes you rich.

'So, where are you from?' Whitney continues.

'New York City.'

'I've been there.'

'Yeah?' I pretend to care.

'YEAH.' She may never stop talking, this occurs to me, and I wonder if I could just ask to stay in detox for a few more weeks, or until the talker goes home. Maybe she'll get tired, or laryngitis.

'My rich mother took me there, before she was too much of a drunk to leave the house.'

'Neat.' I smile. 'Well, we've got something in common, we've both been to New York City. Stellar.'

'Do you know where Bloomingdale's is?'

'Do I?'

'Yeah, have you ever heard of Bloomingdales?'

'Yes, I've heard of Bloomingdales.'

'My grandmother took me there before she died.'

'Touching, really.'

She picks up the lighter brown bag and throws it on the cart.

'Careful. My Walkman's in there.'

'Don't worry, you can't use your Walkman on the unit anyway.'

This means there will be nothing, nothing to drown out the talker. She starts to push the cart out though the door.

'Got everything?'

'Yeah.' We walk through the detox. The nurses wave and smile like it's a parade.

We walk past Cast Man. I wave at him, but he doesn't look up. His eyes reflect the pattern on the TV.

'CCome OOOn. You're not allowed to talk to boys.' She pushes her hair behind her ears and is almost pretty.

'OOOOOOKKKKK.'

'So . . .' I know what's coming, from the inflection of her voice, from the pause in her voice, from the drawn-out way she waits to finish the question. 'So, what was your drug of choice?'

There it is, THE REHAB QUESTION. The most asked, most telling, most requested rehab question. It's the perfect question: they can size you up, figure out what you're about, where you come from, how bad you are, or were. If I had answered Crystal Meth, she'd have known immediately I hung out with truck drivers, probably sold my body and must have left the island of Manhattan to at the very least cop. If I had said I shot dope, we'd have an instant bond, we could talk about needles, veins, and methadone. Saying I snorted blow makes me a lightweight, the quintessential Manhattan rehaber.

'Well,' she continues not waiting for an answer, 'it must have been pretty bad because, you've been in detox for a week.'

'Really? It doesn't seem like a week, it seems like seven days.' I laugh to myself.

'YYYeahhhh. A week is the longest I've known anyone to be in detox.'

We walk together, our strides in synch, through corridors made of big glass windows, past a group of boring social worker types with two pairs of reading glasses each. 'So how much longer are you here?'

'One more week,' she says gleefully.

'Do you know my friend Julia?'

'Yeah. She's my roommate.' I can't see Whitney

having anything to talk to Julia about, except track marks. 'How do you know Julia?'

'Well.' I smile. 'We met at a party at the Museum of Modern Art.'

'I've been there.'

'Really.'

'Julia's leaving tomorrow.' Her voice feels like an intrusion. 'But we're having her medallion services tonight so you'll be there to say goodbye to her.' I wonder what kind of medallions, steak? Venison?

She touches my arm.

'Don't touch me.' Only Jeff touches me. Maybe Janice. No, I'm not crazy, it's just that only dead people can touch me – and they say I need therapy.

'Fine, Miss Touchy.'

'Just stop talking about it, OK?'

'Here we are home sssweet home.' She pushes the glass doors open. 'Welcome to your new home, for twenty-eight days. The time just flies by.'

I look around. Some 'girls' are playing cards on a flimsy round wooden table, like my grand-mother, who plays bridge on the fake bamboo tables in the Palm Beach Country Club's card room. One of the women has black teeth, the other has small nubs for teeth. I try not to stare. Where are the celebrities, the dry cleaners, and the spa treatments? Maybe I should have gone to Betty Ford.

'Come on. It's gonna be just fine. Gonna be fine.' She takes my hand, squeezes it tightly and leads me down the hall.

'So, Ms Miranda. This is to be your room.' She points to the closest door, pushes it open. I walk in behind her, pretending to be confident. There are four beds in the room.

'I thought they had private rooms. Where's the fax machine?' They can't expect me to live this way.

'Nope. No private rooms, no fax machines, no mini-bar.'

'But. Four people in a room?' I tilt my head. She looks at me sideways.

'Don't worry. I had the same response. Swwweeety. You'll be just fine. Jjjust ffffine.' She tosses the bags on the ground and is gone as quickly as she appeared.

I sit down on the bed. The quilt is made from thin plaid polyester that makes an indent when I sit on it. Long lines meet each other in a queasy-making, meltable Mondian pattern.

'Hi.'

I jump. The lump in Bed A begins to move. A corner of white face pokes out from under the comforter, attached to that face is a mass of red frizzy hair. Her arms emerge first then her bare upper torso. 'I'm Bee. Are you new? Did Jesus save you too?'

'Sorry, no. I must have had my cell phone off when he tried to call.'

I hope this is better than sleep-away camp. Bee rises from underneath the polyester floral comforter. She's naked. Her chest is covered in small red marks, healing burns. She walks over to the dresser stiff-legged like she has no knees. She pulls a white cotton eyelet nightie from the top drawer, slides it across her white naked body, a mass of bone.

'So where are you from, Bee?' I pull a wool sweater, a tennis racket, a racket ball racket, a kayaking oar (what was Brett thinking?), and four taffeta ball gowns out of my suitcase (in case I have to be a bridesmaid at a moment's notice).

'The city.'

'Yeah. Me too.' She's sitting on her bed; a wasted wayward angel not that old but probably done with this life, crack smoke for a halo. 'So what's your drug of choice?' Like I even need to ask.

'Crack.' Her eyes are focused on the green shag carpeting. 'I was in a coma for . . .' Bee looks like she's about thirty-five, maybe a little younger. 'It's really because of my sister. I'm getting my lawyer to take me home soon. My driver's picking me up tomorrow. My sister's trying to take my money. She's such a bitch.'

I have fifteen sweaters, twenty-five pairs of underwear, twelve pairs of socks and my roommate is *mashugah*.

'Heavy.' Detox conversations are like the second half of a daytime soap opera or the end of a dinner party when everybody's run out of stories.

'My mother and father are in France. But when they come home then . . . then . . . They say my parents are dead. But they . . . they don't know. They don't know. I do.'

'So . . .'

She smiles while we chat; she's begun to eat white chocolate methodically. There's chocolate on her hands, on the chair, and under her finger-nails. She's focused, gotta give her that: nothing distracts her from her candy.

The room is a rectangle with two beds across from each other, small plastic tables, and the mandatory plastic flowers. The girl in bed B has put up posters of rock stars and Leo DeCaprio. It just gets more and more pathetic.

'So are they . . . are they dead?'

'Yeah. I mean no. Well.' Bee looks like she'd be more comfortable in *The Shining*, than the rehab. 'I don't know. After the car accident things became really hard to understand. I was in a coma for three months. Three months. I was supposed to be dead, but I'm not.' She says in a voice that's a monotone hum.

'So where in the city did you grow up?' Story of my life, trying to act normal in the face of what-ever this is.

'1150 Fifth. And the H . . . Hamptons.'

'Yeah. I grew up on East Eighty-Fifth Street.'

'Do you know who my family is?' With an intro-duction like that . . .

'I only know your first name.'

'My father is Andy Rossenger.' The very famous, the very dead Andy Rossenger.

'*Sacra*,' I say, picturing her hair straight, her face covered in cream colored make-up, her bones poured into a Bob Macki, feathers and all. It is in that picture, in that recreated image, that I recognize her. Her freckles obscured by airbrush, placed in the society pages of *Avenue*, *Quest*, and other great pieces of social propaganda.

It must have been three years ago, in a much publicized car accident, that Bee's parents went off the Grand Corniche, like Grace Kelly had only a few decades before. But Grace Kelly was a princess and Andy Rossenger wasn't a prince, just another rich drunk, who killed his mistress in a car accident. I saw his twisted mess of a Jaguar in a fifteen-second clip spliced between advertisements for tampons.

'So, so so,' she sings, as she putters in the little wooden chest of drawers. 'So, so.' As she pulls out another chocolate bar and begins to make more noise with its wrapper. 'So. Where did you go to school?'

'Dayton, Riverfield, and Hemsly. I graduated from Hemsly.' Secret meaning: I'm not as rich as my watch would lead you to believe and I'm Jewish.

'Oh, I went to Dalegate, the girls' school on Ninety-Third Street.'

'I know it well.' At least I know something.

'I graduated in eighty-three. Did you know Dina Kahn, my Jewish friend?'

Of course I'd know your Jewish friend because all Jewish people in New York are friends, and we all go to this room where we control the banks and the media.

Hemsly, where I graduated from, is known as the school for rich semi-stupid Jews. The smart Jews go to Dayton, where I was gracelessly asked to leave. And the hopelessly stupid, the clique that took their SATs in crayon, go to Riverfield. 'Kahn? No.'

'You're Jewish.'

'How did you know?'

'You look it.' Is it the prayer shawl that gives me away?

'I haven't looked around.' I glance up at her. 'I would like to meet the others.' But would I really? No, probably not.

She lies back in the bed, as if she never really got out. She begins to snore. I look at the sweaters, some date back to seventh grade, others earlier. They vary in color from dark brown to black. I sit down on the bed and it sinks.

I lie on the bed, close my eyes and pretend to be dead.

Next thing I know a girl enters the room like a tornado, her face is in a scrunch, her body is compressed by her angry posture.

'New Girl!' She leers.

'Yeahhhhh.' I pretend she has woken me from my pseudo-sleep.

'So, what's your story?'

'My story?'

'Oh, you know. What was your drug of choice. Blah, blah, blah.'

'I just had a little problem with blow. But everyone who does coke has a problem with it.'

'Yeah, yeah sure.'

'What was your drug of choice?'

'I just had a little problem with sticking needles in my arms.' She begins to laugh.

'I know who you are.' Simon Woke's daughter, party girl, A-lister? She looks at me nervously. 'You're the week-in-detox-girl right?' Or that.

'Yeah. Can you take me somewhere to smoke?'

'For the week-in-detox-girl, anything. I'm Beth, by the way.' We walk on the green shag carpet past the grey double-faced cotton drapes to the white plastic-chaired smoking section.

'Week-in-detox-girl meet Midge and Kim.' Beth takes a plastic chair near the big round tin ashtray. She motions to the empty seat like she likes me. The hail rains so hard it takes me three tries to light my cigarette. And you think cigarettes aren't addictive.

'Hi Midge.' Midge is shaped like a swollen toad. She has twigs for arms, buttons for eyes, a bloated torso and no teeth.

'What's your name?' Midge opens her mouth, Midge has fewer teeth than I thought.

'Week-in-detox-girl.' Beth blurts.

'Actually it's Miranda.'

'Nice to meetcha.'

'I'm Kim.' Kim is huge, at least 3000 pounds. She smiles and I am relieved to see she has teeth. Where are the famous patients?

We sit and freeze. Our smoke mixes in the soft waves of gray discolored light. No one says anything. One cigarette dissolves into another. 'What was your drug of choice, Miranda?'

'Oh, she's just a visitor. You know. She's here by mistake.'

'Yeah.' They all giggle. Beth looks at Midge and Kim and laughs even more.

'Alcohol.' My tongue gets stuck on that exquisite word. '. . . Coke. Heroin. Valium. Morphine. Demerol. Percoset. Crack. Klonopin.' I smile. They look at me. Silence. Beth looks shocked. 'And Xanax, Vodka, Halcyon, Tylenol number three, and Pot.'

'All at once. Yeah?' Midge looks at me with wide eyes.

'All at once.'

'Wow.'

'I'm a chemist.'

'Sure are.' Beth pats me on the back like I've passed the initiation, and now they'll like me. I light another cigarette and lean back knowing I've won.

'It's Kim's second time here in two months.' Beth talks to me but looks at Midge.

'Yeah, Kim's heading out to the halfway house in St Paul tomorrow. She's gonna spend a long time there.' Midge clearly is the talker.

'You on librium?'

'No.' I shake my shaky head at her. 'Serax.'

'Serax. Yeah?' Midge says.

'Yeah.'

'Serax.' Beth chimes in introspectively, as if we'd said something really deep.

'You're like one of those over-privileged rich kids from New York City. One of those intellectual types who complains about migrant farmers and immigrants, all the while pretending to be a liberal.'

I've never heard a better description of my family. 'No.'

'I just don't understand how this happened to me,' I say.

'Take a number.' Midge looks up at the sky.

'Why did this happen to me?'

Beth frowns. 'Why not you? Why not you, Miranda Woke?'

And I get it, for the first time in my life I get it. I'm a drug addict same as Beth, Midge, and Kim. I close my eyes and the realization comes to me, not because I want it to, just because it does. I'm going to die if I drink or use drugs again. I'm going to end up in a pine box next to Jeff, as dead as he is, if I drink again.

chapter ten

chapter 10

Call me crazy, but there's no place I'd rather have Thanksgiving than rehab. I'm surprised but I really like being here, more than being with my family in some hotel lobby drinking red wine out of big hand-blown glasses and pretending everything's OK. You'd think it would be the other way around, but sitting at a long tan wooden table, surrounded on either side by junkies at various stages of detox – some still sweating and shaking, others incoherent, spilling food all over their sweaters – seems so much more natural.

The meal is a parody of fine dining: plastic knives, thick institutional porcelain plates, and dry turkey. I sit next to Beth, who should have left weeks ago but has chosen to stay because she has no place to go.

There's fifteen feet of snow on the ground. The green sweater my father's secretary sent me to ward off the cold is both too long (to my knees) and too small (arms too short) for me. I think it's really a child's dress.

The cranberry sauce is the type that has been slid right out of the can and then mashed up so it looks like it was made fresh. Though why anyone would want fresh cranberry sauce, or even to pretend to have fresh cranberry sauce, is a mystery to me. Beth looks at me with a mouthful of food.

'See, food.' She opens her mouth to show it full of unchewed food. The rest of the table starts to giggle.

'Ha. Nice. Really mature,' I say. But Margaret, who's sitting to my right, laughs in appreciation.

Margaret is the first person who understands that my dull universe is the place where self-loathing blends with sitcoms, and dullness like Vaseline coats everything I see. She's the first person I've ever really liked who wasn't me. She's become my rehab mate, my best friend.

Margaret's mother is a Texas socialite, who sent her daughter to Hazelford instead of to camp.

'What are you thinking about?' Margaret has a soft voice.

'Nothing.' I stick my fork in my watery mashed potatoes.

'Oh, is that right?'

'You betcha,' I say in my best Minnesota accent, drawing a line through my mashed potatoes with the tines of my fork.

'Mirrrranddddda.' She pulls the skin off her dry turkey. 'Do you want to go for a walk after this?'

'Sure, it's not like there's anything else to do here.'

'We could hang ourselves.' Margaret laughs.

'No bed-sheets.' I smile at her.

'You two are so fucking depressing. Like a morose funeral,' Beth says.

'Somebody's going home.' Beth looks at me and then points to Kim who is finally going home, graduating from forty-nine days in a twenty-eight-day program. Kim is carrying out a long Hazelford tradition, walking through the cafeteria banging a pot and a spoon together in perfect toneless junky harmony. Toneless junky harmony.

'Wow.' Margaret looks at Kim with indescribable envy.

'She gets to go home. I on the other hand will most likely be here FOR THE REST OF MY LIFE!

'Not true. Let's go.' Margaret gets up and starts to walk away.

'Wait.' I grab ten Crisco-y cookies for the road.

Our feet drag the way they do when junkies observe nature.

As we walk, my mind returns to the tape that keeps playing over and over: *'Will I drink again? If I drink again will I die? Could I still drink beer? I never really got drunk on beer. Could I take one Valium? Maybe I could handle heroin. Maybe I could do that. Can I ever drink again? Could I go to one of those places where they teach you to drink safely? Am I really an alcoholic? I mean I'm only nineteen years old. Did we share needles? Did Jeff really have AIDS? Will I get AIDS?'*

'If you're talking to yourself, you're talking to the wrong person.' Margaret runs her boots though the snow, the frost and below that, the leaves.

'What if I have AIDS?'

'You don't have AIDS.'

'How do you know?'

'Well, I don't know for sure. But I bet you don't. They'll do a test in a week. But I've shot dope since I was twelve, which is like—' She sighs, looking through the file cabinet in her brain. 'That's like almost eight years, and I don't have it.'

I kiss her on the cheek. Her cheek feels very warm.

Please, I changed my mind, I want to come back.

'We're gonna make it. Right?'

'I don't know.'

'Fuck you.'

'Forgive me for not being able to predict the future.'

'Well, I'd like to speak with the person who can.'

'I'll arrange it.'

'Thanks.' She laughs. Our giggles fill the woods, reverberate off the snow, and are held here in this clearing.

Margaret is being kicked out. My counselor, Mary, comes into the room to tell me this.

'But why?' I lie on my bed like every teenager from the dawn of time, flopping my head from side to side.

'She'll tell you.'

What's going to happen to her? Where's she going to go? 'Do you think I'm going home soon?'

'Yeah.' She smiles. 'We're sending you home next week.'

'Yeah? Home for Christmas?'

'I thought you were Jewish.' Mary looks at me puzzled.

'Culturally, yes. So when next week?'

'Next Tuesday. But,' she gives me a small, some-what coy smile 'but, we are suggesting you live with your mother.'

'WHAT?'

'Truth.' Mary talks like a *Sweet Valley High* novel. 'What could you people possibly be thinking? She'll do much better if she lives with her Valium addicted neurotic crazed socialite mother. Her very sane codependent (learning the lingo of recovery) mother, who sometimes thinks she's Lana Turner.'

'Why don't you come with me.' She walks out the door; I follow her, walking so closely that I can smell her Charlie perfume. We head into her office, a giant incarnation of a Hallmark card, decked with teddy bears and flowery platitude-filled plaques. She sits behind her high desk and peers over a pile of papers at me.

'Your mother says she wants you to live with her.'

'What?'

'Yeah, and your father called me.' She steamrolls

along. A feeling of rage rises up in me. Hasn't he punished me enough, now to come in at the fifth act? Perfect.

'What?'

'Your father wants you to come live with him in Paris. I think he wants another chance at being a father. He seems really nice. He also sounded sad, like he really misses you.'

'Well he always SEEMS sad. That's his thing.'

'Both of them want you.'

'Well they sure have an impressive way of showing it.'

'What can I say?'

'You've said enough.'

'I think you should take some time. Ask yourself what it is you want and need.'

'Fine.'

The door to Mary's office makes an unsatisfying slam; it's too thin, not heavy enough to make any noise.

As I look back at them, my cocaine nights are suspended in slow motion like pieces of memories that you have to squint to see. It had all become a joke, and after that, Jeff had fallen off the flat edge of the world. I knew I wasn't far behind him, treading water in my mother's pool, killing time.

Now as it's all gotten further away, I realize that all hell of that nature is essentially the same. All of it, like every grain of sand in a vast desert is about shame. Sometimes they would tell her she had no shame, but the nineteen-year-old coke whore was filled with shame, at her core, in the way she saw everything around her. The kind of shame that can only come from a mixture of a father who was long gone, a lifetime of being called a beast, and a feeling in her gut of never being quite right.

I feel like I've been here forever.

Margaret is going home. She looks very different in outside garb. I've never seen her with make-up on; she looks like Tami Fay Baker has assaulted her with black plastic eyelashes and a dump truck filled with oily peach foundation.

'So, tough girl. Where to now?' My eyes move down her body. She's wearing a tight shirt, the kind purchased for seduction.

'Maybe back to Boston. I have some friends in Boston. I don't want to go back to Texas. I want to start a new life. I need to be someplace different.' She sighs as if she was discussing a dream but that's always my mistake, thinking the truth is poetic when in reality, it's pathetic. 'I need to go someplace where I'll be safe.'

'You have no idea how much I'm going to miss you.'

'Yeah.'

'You've become such a part of my life.' My shrink says my problem is that I treat everyone as if they are replaceable.

'Yeah.'

'Margaret, can I ask you something?'

'Shoot.' She drags on her hand-rolled cigarette, rubbing her blue hand against her sweater.

'Why did they ask you to leave?'

'What?'

'Why did they ask you to leave?'

'They found some pills in my bag.'

'Have you been using?'

'Yeah.'

'How could you do this to me?' I feel completely deflated, like she punched me in the chest. Maybe she doesn't know that there's something better. I wish I could tell her, but that's not the way this works.

chapter eleven

Packing is not going so well. I stand up, assessing the situation. The large oval face of a racket-ball racket sticks out of the back pocket of my green mesh suitcase. The sad truth of all of this is that I didn't play racket ball once.

I hear my name on the speaker paging me to Mary's office.

I go into her office with my bare feet dragging underneath me.

'Well.' She sits behind her desk. I take a peppermint candy out of the white plastic jar on her desk and unwrap it. She hands me a copper coin with hands imprinted on it. 'Here is your medallion and you deserve it. I'm glad you stayed for ten weeks instead of four.' She passes the coin from the palm of her hand to the palm of mine.

'But I'm still sweating, still detoxing after ten weeks, I have a constant headache and, while I want to stay sober, most of me feels like I'll be back here in a few weeks.'

'You'll be OK, just go to meetings.'

A man who I've never seen in my ten weeks here comes to help me with my bags. He is really cute, tall, bony, gaunt. Just my type, love those anorexic men. He puts my suitcases on a cart and wheels them down the hallway. I walk behind the cart. I smile at the people I pass. Midge and Kim have left weeks ago; Margaret's probably smoking crack and shooting dope. Bee however is still here, winning the prize as the longest inpatient in Hazelford, eleven weeks and counting. She waves at me, handing me one of her business cards and promising she'll be back in the city soon, and maybe then we can meet for a drink or something. I don't think Bee's figured out why she's here. A lot of people who I've only known for a few days or less wave and look at me in awe. I feel like the mayor of this little town in purgatory.

When I get to La Guardia, Brett is waiting for me even though I told him not to pick me up. He's lost some weight, but none of that seems to matter, the sight of him infuriates me. I don't want it to, I want to just fall into his arms and tell him I love him and always have, but I know that's way beyond what I can do. It's the way he stands there, smiling, mispronouncing every word in the dictionary; saying 'idear' instead of 'idea' fills me with rage.

'Thanks for picking me up.' I fling my heavy carry-on at him.

'No hug?'

I try to hug him, and slip away quickly to look for my bags on the carousel.

'Well Randa, I'm glad you're back, even if you're weird.'

'Thanks.' It's noisy in the airport. I put my fingers in my ears. Brett essentially frosts mattresses for a living and the cold has made all the cake frosting in New York too stiff to work with so he has nothing to do for the rest of the winter.

'I missed you, Miranda.'

'Yeah.'

'I mean miss you. I miss you. Where did the Miranda I know go?'

And I get lost in every crowd, try to gloss over all of this, to put everyone in my boxes. But I can't make him anything else than what he is and he's right, our window is closing. He doesn't recognize me anymore and I don't either.

'Let's just get the bags. OK?'

The car floats down the highway like an unfrosted mattress. We drive down East Sixty-Fifth Street. A light dusting of newly fallen snow coats the street. Everything looks flawless, picturesque, perfect. I feel like a giant blemish on the face of the Upper East Side.

The houses on Sixty-Fifth Street blur together and look like one giant shiny limestone brick. All these rich people in such a small space, meeting each other at dinner parties, sleeping with each other's wives, swapping lives with each other. I bet no one wants to swap with me.

My childhood bedroom is as it always was. Purple floral Laura Ashley wallpaper still hangs, and dull offwhite shades still clap when they roll up too high to pull them back down. The pillows used to be lavender but are faded from the sun. Everything else is frozen. It's the way Mom shows me she loves me, keeping everything the same as it once was like I might come back. And now here I am, back with nothing to show for myself. 'Where's Mom?' Of course Mom misses the homecoming.

'Not here. Can I ask you something?'

'Sure,' I say.

'Why didn't you go live with your father?'

'Because he didn't really want me. I just know that. What am I going to do with my life? What am I going to do for work? School?'

'You never worried about those things before. Besides. your parents have money.'

'That's not the point. What kind of life is that being supported by your parents. Where's the life in that?'

'Who is that talking, *Where's the life? Where's the life?* That doesn't sound like the Miranda Woke I know.'

'This is me.'

'Sure.'

'Come on, Brett. You have a job don't you?'

'I'm a painter.' He lies back on the bed.

'I know, but a job that earns you money.'

'I wait tab . . .' He stops. I smile at him.

'I can't hear you, Brett. What did you say?'

'I'm a waiter.'

'Well, I need to go back to school, because I don't want to be a waitress.'

'Come on Rand, don't worry about it right now. Maybe you should rest for a while.'

I get up to go to the bathroom. Brett's ordered at least a hundred dollars' worth of pork buns and we are anxiously awaiting their arrival. The bottles that sit on the edge of the sink are coated with a thin film of dust. There is a large plastic bottle of rubbing alcohol on the sink. I love the radicalness of drinking rubbing alcohol. Kitty Dukakis did it all the time; I saw her do it in her TV biography. I look at the bottle, the mouth of the bottle, the way the liquid clings to the sides of the neck. If it's good enough for the wife of a presidential candidate, it's good enough for me. I twist off the top of the bottle and smell before I pour the contents of the plastic bottle down the sink. The phone starts ringing as the bottle thumps in the metal wastebasket.

I walk into the empty bedroom off the bathroom. I pick up the phone. The mouthpiece is dusty. Charming. Hasn't Mom ever heard of Dust-Off?

'Hello.' Hoping it's Mom, calling to welcome me home.

'Hello, is this Miranda?'
'Yeah.' I sit down on the bed where my nanny used to sleep. Another untouched room in this hideous wax museum filled with sculptures made of wax.
'Miranda, this is Mary Post. Do you remember me? I'm your mom's friend from college. I was at the Christmas party.'
Was I?
'Your mother asked me if I would call you. I thought I might take you to a meeting. I've been saving you a seat in AA for a long time.' She laughs.
'Saving me a seat?'
'You'll see.'

chapter twelve

I feel like hell – achey, empty, and discontent. I had hoped that being spared would feel better. Today, I'm exactly ten weeks sober. Cocaine, heroin, diet pills, alcohol, and etc are out of my blood; all that's left is Valium. Doctors say Valium withdrawal lasts somewhere between three months and two years.

'Brett, will you go down to the kitchen and see if there are any doughouts down there?'

'You finished all of them last night.'

'But there were twenty in that box.' I'm lying under three layers of blankets in a bed from my mother's first marriage, in my mother's lazily decorated house filled with furniture from every marriage and every year of the 'eighties.

'And now there are none.'

'Fine. I'll go buy some more later.'

I lean over the side of the bed and pick up my cigarettes in their white plastic box.

'Do you need a light?'

He sits at the foot of the bed, heavy on my feet,

floating around the edge of the bed like a little blip, a used sound-bite.

'No, I'll use two rocks, Cro-Magnon man.'

'You are a prize. How did I get so lucky?'

'Odds, timing. I need a light.' Half hanging off the bed, I look up at him. He reaches down and lights my cigarette with the lighter he carries expressly for me.

'Thanks. You know I think you're cool.' That was one of the stupidest phrases ever uttered to another person in the hopes of not having to say love.

'So when is Mary coming?'

'Nine-thirty. I think.' I suck on the plastic filter of my cigarette. I love smoking.

'Not to upset you. But we have to talk about something . . .' No good news has ever followed that sentence.

'Janice's called eleven times. She wants to see you. She misses you. She loves you. I think she's a horrible influence on you. That said, I think you should call her back.'

'Why?' I pull a black sweater out of the drawer. It's not a particularly nice sweater; it looks like the kind of thing you'd buy on the street but it's by Helmut Lang. 'I thought you said you thought she was a bad influence.'

I pull the sweater over my head.

'God . . . Miranda, give me a fucking break for once in my life. Everybody's talking about you, I can't keep lying to them. Nobody buys this story that you've been writing at your parents' horse farm in Minnesota for ten weeks.'

'Why not?'

'Because everybody knows why New Yorkers like you go to Minnesota.'

He turns towards me, catching me on my way into the closet. Grasping me in one of his giant bonecrushing hugs. There is something wonderfully comforting about the way Brett smells, like Secret antiperspirant for women, toothpaste, and my second-hand smoke.

Mary Post is the same as she always was, short and thin, thin, thin, the way rich women who lunch are thin, like they've hit the Laysix too hard. MP has long brown hair, the kind that belongs on someone half her age and that looks uncomfortable on someone who's floating in the well-preserved fifty-plus zone. She has no kids, a billionaire husband, and a hot pink sweater set that proves aggression and etiquette can coexist.

'Wow! It's great to see you, Mary.' I smile at her. 'Do you want to come in?' She glances at my black sweater and jeans that have fringed cuffs instead of hems.

'No. I think we should go if we want to be there on time.' Mary Post is walking like she'll be late for the first race at Ascot if the Saatchis keep her too long lecturing on the genius of Damien Hirst – basically the woman oozes non-Judaism from every pore. Now don't get me wrong. I like her and everything. I'm just placing her, for clarity's sake.

'Where's your mother?' That's the ten million-dollar question.

'Brett?' I look at him standing on the steps.

'She'll be back in a couple of weeks. She's in China, hiking, then coming home via Europe.' His eyes focus on Mary's pearls, shiny golf balls.

'Will you be here when I get back?' He nods. Yes, he'll wait for me. Was there ever any question?

'Good,' I say, following Mary Post out the door.

I feel like it's the first day of school. Mary Post in her white fur coat, me in my parka, looking up and down the street at the businessmen walking to work and the children going to school. If I were still partying I'd just be coming home right now – coming home and coming down.

'How are you feeling?' Mary Post says.

'Not great.'

'Well, what does that mean?' She turns to me. Her face opens up in a sort of half smile.

'I'm so tired. I feel so exhausted and I don't understand why. A Valium detox feels like having your face smashed in with a baseball bat and then trying to apply make-up over it.'

'Well, darling.' Mary can make even the word darling feel genuine. 'That was what it was like for me in the beginning. When I was detoxing from Valium, I felt the same way.' Mary Post does not look like the kind of woman who should use detoxing in a sentence, and she certainly doesn't look like the kind of woman who should be using it to describe herself.

'Yeah?' I'm just sort of walking behind her, awaiting further instructions.

'The bad part is over.'

'I don't know why people keep saying that to me. I certainly don't feel like the bad part's over.'

'You're about to embark on a beautiful journey.' Beautiful journey, God, spirituality, and The Path . . . God I can handle, though what the journey is, spiritualism may be, The Path is and where it goes is a mystery to me. 'And I will be there with you the whole way, darling.' I realize I want Mary Post as a traveling companion, even if I have no idea what it is she's talking about.

'You're going to be OK. Just trust.' She puts her hand on my cheek. It's warm from the mink-lined pockets of her coat. 'I promise.' She pauses. 'Just take it easy.'

'What?' Sucking back on my cigarette, I wonder if people are becoming more cryptic or if I've finally destroyed the logic brain cells that bounce around in my head.

There's no point in describing an AA meeting: it's like a car accident or the Grand Canyon, always lost in the translation.

Mary Post walks me uptown. She takes my hand the way people do in off-color 'seventies movies where everyone's dying of cancer.

'I have this horrible feeling that all my choices were like martini olives made in the context of alcohol. I'm going to have to start over again.'

Mary Post gives me a hug. 'Yes, but remember you're not the first to start over.' Then she, and her cashmere twin set, walk west to her fourteen-room apartment on Park Avenue.

'I'll pick you up same time tomorrow.' I feel a little better after the meeting.

I continue up Lexington Avenue, dragging myself past the liquor store, fighting that magnetic pull. The little alcoholic voice in my head sings for the old days of Wild Turkey and vomiting on my mother. Only an alcoholic would miss the days of vomiting on family members.

I walk into the bookstore. I don't even really read – maybe the occasional piece of poetry and everything by Fay Weldon. No one in my family reads. No, no one in my family reads or thinks: they'd get a headache, reach for the Advil, trip on their twelve thousand-dollar Burken handbag and smash their heads into their Sub-Zero refrigerators. No, books are too dangerous, no point in wasting a life over them.

'Hi, Max.' Mac's prestigious Upper East Side education has guaranteed him a lifetime of running a bookstore.

'Hey, Miranda Woke.' I like him even though he talks into his shirt pocket and always ends our conversations abruptly with a resounding, 'Well, good to hear you're doing well.' Which makes me think he hasn't heard a word I've said.

'Your father was in here a few weeks ago.'

'Wasn't him. He's in Paris.'

'No, it was him, credit card and all. Said he was here for an opening. You were with him, no? I saw your picture in the *Observer*.'

'No. That was his wife, but I could understand how you might think it was me, after all she's only three years older than I am.'

'Ohh. Sorry.'

'My father and I are not exactly close. We haven't talked to each other in a few years.'

'Sorry. Didn't mean to bring up a sore subject

'He's the least of my problems right now.'

I'm lying on my lavender carpet staring at the TV. The show 'Diff'rent Strokes' is blaring. Dana Plato died of an OD two nights ago but on TV she looks like any happy sixteen-year-old, frozen in sitcom land for the rest of time with all the other famous dead people.

'Do you want to go to Void tonight? There's a big party for that photographer, what's-his-name.' Brett's eating a bagel with cream cheese, what else is there to do when you're young, Jewish and without a mattress to frost.

'I don't need to go to Void. I live in the Void. I am the Void.'

'Well, no one would argue with that, Randa. But it might be a good time to make an appearance, to explain to those people where you've been, that I haven't murdered you and left you in a shallow grave marked only by a twig somewhere in upstate New York not far from the highway.'

'Hummmm.'

'Yeah. Besides it's a really A-list kinda thing. Everyone will be there.'

'Well, maybe I'll go. Make a declaration of my sanity and then leave. I think I should call Mary Post and ask her what to do.'

'Now you need permission to go to a party?'

Void is in a basement on the part of Mercer Street that is lined with cobblestones instead of pavement, and despite Mary's suggestion not to, I'm here, walking down the blue plastic steps.

The only thing that makes Void different from all the other clubs is its bright yellow floor. 'Can I get you a Diet Coke, Randa?' There is something particularly grimy about clubs in sobriety. For the first time I can see the dirt – bottle caps, cigarette butts, dust bunnies on the floor – and smell the odor of stale beer.

'With lime, Brett, and watch him pour it. Make sure it's only Diet Coke. Would you?' I still don't know how I feel about Brett, but a level of comfort has set in, making it hard for me to imagine life without him.

'Miranda Woke, where have you been?' Whit says, assaulting me with the smells of whiskey, Preparation-h, and cigars, which seem to escape from his pores, from every orifice of his body.

'Hospitalized from my last OD.'

'OH.' It's a little soon to say, but I think I won this conversation.

'Yeah. Look here's my scar from the IV. wish they didn't slam it so far into the veins.'

'Well, we're glad to have you back.' We who?

I turn. A suit, Arab looking, perfectly dressed, groomed within an inch of his life, stands in the doorway. He is immediately out of place.

Janice appears through the door in a silver dress with an Arab man wrapped around one arm.

We were all thinking . . . my god. He stops, puts his hand on my stomach like I'm pregnant. 'Miranda, did you put on some weight?'

'A little.' I look down at my stomach, convex where it was once concave. 'Well, a lot I guess.'

'I would say.'

'Thanks. Really.' I try to suck in my stomach, but the truth is that I'm looking more and more like Monica Lewinsky every day. It's the Jewish girl's crisis diet: frozen yogurt and muffins. 'Look, there's Janice,' I whisper into his stubble. 'Who's she with?'

'I would guess from the look of it . . . a friendly banker.'

'Do you know his name? Is he NOSS (New on the Social Scene)?'

'No, I don't think so. I think he's a visitor.'

'As to be expected, typical new-boy syndrome. We know how this goes.'

Janice booms down the steps in her seven-inch pumps. She sees me and runs over and jumps on me like a puppy.

'Is that Miranda Woke, the girl who fell off the earth, missing in partying action?'

'Hi, Janice.'

'Darling, darling, sweetheart, gorgeous. Ohhhh my god. How long? How long?' She's so excited to see me she could pop a vein (if she has any left) or dislodge some more collagen.

'A long time,' I say as she kisses me lightly on each cheek.

'I missed you, darling. I have NEFSOF (News from the Social Front). Lots. And I've been calling you.'

'Yeah?' She twirls her banker around her arm like a pashmina but richer. 'Have you met my banker, I mean John?'

'No.'

'John is my new favorite boy.'

'Hi,' he says.

'Hi.'

'It's been sooo long. James left me. Gone, darling, back to mommy and daddy. He'll come back though, always does.' With that the banker turns to her. 'Oh, don't worry it's not what it sounds like. Right, Randa?' She smiles at me; I'm still lost somewhere in the beginning of her monologue – if only she had kept her monologue internal.

'No. But . . .'

'Oh and I'm the co-chair with the real power for this benefit at the Gug. Should be fun, babe.'

'Sure.'

'What's the matter?'

'I need to talk to you.'

'Where?' We look around the club. It's dark but every inch is filled with people and party noise, that half-speak/half-laugh gibberish that goes on when all the guests have had just enough wine to lubricate them into conversation.

'Bathroom.'

'But I heard you didn't do that anymore. Or are you back?'

'No, I'm not back. God, considering you told me to go to rehab, I'd think you'd be just the slightest bit supportive.' She rolls her eyes at me. 'I just have to ask you one thing. One tiny thing. Here.' I point to the door over the steps. 'Let's go outside. That's probably the best idea.'

She follows me up the steps and out the large grey door. We stand on the cobblestones under the street lamp.

'It's been so long. So much to catch up with, my god. DDDDAAAAARRRLLLLIIInnnnggg.' She gives me a quick squeeze.

'Did Jeff have AIDS?'

'I don't really see how that's relevant to anything, do you? Besides, now that he's offed himself all that other stuff isn't of any importance.'

'OK. Are you sure Jeff killed himself?'

'Yeah, why?'

'Well is it possible that I could have killed him?' She looks at me with this sort of fashionable southern shock, like she's dropped her hypodermic in a friend's mint julep.

'No. You didn't kill Jeff.' She stops. 'I can hardly imagine you killing anything let alone Jeff.' She says it like a put-down. The banker steps out onto the street.

'I know. I'm nuts, right?'

'Darling. Have you entirely taken leave? You didn't kill anyone. Why would you even think that?'

'I'm crazy.'

'Listen, we have another party to go to.' She smiles at the banker. He doesn't say anything; he just stands there like he's made of wax, which he probably is. Another Duane Hanson in a life made up of them.

'Are you sure?'

'Without question, darling, without question.' She leans into me, so close I can smell the vodka on her breath. It smells sharp, cold. 'Sometimes people kill themselves. My father killed himself.'

'I didn't know that.'

'Yes, you did.'

'I'm sorry.'

'Sometimes people kill themselves, and the rest of us are left to wonder why. Stop wondering, Randa. Don't give yourself too much credit with this one. This great love that you think you had, well . . .'

'Well what?'

'Well, just, it's just that I don't think you were the only person to get attached to him. Do you get where I'm going with this?'

'No.'

'He loved you the way he loved everyone. You're young, you'll understand this some day. Some men are like that.'

'What do you mean?'

'Randa, if he were alive today, he wouldn't be able to remember your name. Let him go. It's better that way. None of it had to do with you.' She looks at the banker; he looks down at his expensive shiny silver watch.

For a second and a lump of cookie dough I think she might be much smarter than I thought. 'OK, we've got to go. But I'll see you really soon, darling, and you're alright, right?'

I look down at my feet.

Without waiting for a response she touches my arm and jumps in a taxi, banker in tow.

'Yeah, I'm fine. I guess.'

chapter thirteen

It's hard to escape in sobriety. Sleep and food are the ways that I try to shut off the voices in my head, the ones that tell me in a million different ways that I'm different, I'm not a good person.

The sober Next-Best-Thing is a better shrink, more AA meetings, a new Melody Beattie book, or the next step.

The phone rings and the first thing I think is that I'm dreaming. When I realize I'm not dreaming, when my eyes open to the flashing red lights on the phone, I half wonder, half wish that it's my mother calling to tell me she's coming home, because I'm lonely and a bit scared by my new life, by the fact I can't even take one Valium. My eyes open and the surface of my skin is coated in sweat. The whole room smells like hot sweaty sleep. All the lights are on. The dark now scares me like it did when I was small. It's two in the morning, and it's not Mom on the other side of the phone.

'Randa, Randa.' James sings into Bob Dylan's

screams and screeches. James's voice is heavy, thick with cigarette phlegm.

'What kind of time difference is there in Boston? 'cause it's two in the morning here in New York. Not exactly regular phoning hours. I'm sleeping.' I pull the comforter around my shoulders. I feel safe in bed with all the lights on, with all my old stuffed animals looking down on me like little guardians.

'With whom?'

'Come on, James.'

'No snide answer? I expect more than that from you, Ms Randa.'

'Come on, James, it's late. I'm too tired for this.'

'Don't you wanna have a little boozy chat, baby?'

'I've been rehabed. Can I call you in the morning?'

'No.'

'Well then, what is it?'

'Randa, this is an emergency. Have you seen my wife?'

'I've been in rehab for ten weeks, James, I haven't exactly been keeping up with the social scene.' I'm still a liar. Some things won't change, not right away, anyway.

'Ohh.' I think about the last time that I saw James. He was dragging me out of some party, I think. I was the mess, the Miranda hurricane of drugs, smudged eye make-up, and chaos, and he was the one who was ambulatory. It's odd how quickly those roles can be reversed.

'Listen, I'm really tired.'

'I'm worried about her. Whit said he saw her earlier on this evening. He said she was with this Arab banker guy, and they got into a limo.'

'I don't understand you. You leave her and then become so obsessed with her every move until you can't stand it anymore, and then go back to her. She always does this, picks up some banker, some visitor to our world, and then she carries on with him in front of you until you go nuts and come back.'

'So?'

'So what? Why leave if you're always gonna go back? I say you should just admit that you're in love with each other in your own highly sick way and get on with it. I mean . . .'

'You'd be far less obnoxious if you acted nineteen instead of thirty.'

'Less obnoxious, but less charming. Willing to make the trade? Anyway I'm not obnoxious.' I light a cigarette.

'Where do you think the two of them went?'

'I don't know.' I really don't.

'So, I'm so self-involved, tell me about you. Are you still obsessed with Jeff? You didn't kill him, you know.'

'I've been told.'

'He was a fucking unstable asshole. None of us ever liked him at all. And he was dying of AIDS.'

I always thought James liked Jeff; I always thought everyone liked Jeff.

'He had AIDS?'

'Well, nobody's sure. But . . .'

'Well, if nobody's sure, then how is that a fact?' Can't they just leave him alone? Why can't I not know?

'It's not. I'm just telling you, the man didn't care if he lived or died. Besides, I know you didn't kill him, because Janice . . . God, Randa you weren't even there when he died. Janice was there, she saw him die. Lovely story really. The touching story of a heroin addict who chokes to death on his own vomit. When she comes back, if she comes back, she'll tell you all about it.'

'But, James. She's off.'

'Yeah, well you know what that's like, Randa.'

'Are you two going to get back together?'

He coughs. 'You really are nineteen. There's so much you don't understand about people. When people have been together as long as Janice and I . . . well, you couldn't understand. You just couldn't. This is the kind of thing only grown-ups understand.'

'I am a grown-up.'

'No, Randa. No you're not. You're nineteen years old, you're a kid.'

'Why don't you just stay in Boston?'

'I'm coming back. The party's in New York.'

'No it's not, James.'

'Just because you got sober doesn't mean the rest of us had problems with drugs.'

'I know.'

'And it doesn't make Janice a heroin addict.'

'Why did you call me?'

'The famous guy died. You know that don't you?'

'Yeah, I know. It's horrible.'

'Isn't it? But he wasn't the nicest guy either.'

'Goodbye, James.'

'I know you think we're bad, but nothing we do is morally wrong. Just because I'm gay, and she might have the smallest thing with drugs, doesn't make us wrong.'

'Go to bed, James.'

'You go on, ride your fucking moral high horse. You're no better than any one of us.'

'I know, James.'

'Don't forget you're a fucking junkie, nineteen-year-old coke whore. You'll go back to it. Don't worry, you'll go back to it. You may be sober but that's just for now. You'll be back to it with a vengeance, sooner than you think.'

'Whatever.'

'Don't think you get to go back to normal life now, Randa. Don't think that. That's a load of crap. The stuff you've seen, that'll fuck you up forever. Yes it will. Twenty years from now, you'll still be thinking about the time you fucked that guy for a hit, or lay on a bathroom floor for hours with a needle hanging out of your arm. People like you don't get well. You'll always be different. You'll always be fucked. Listen, Janice's been sober, she's always gone back and so will you.'

'Goodnight, James.'

'You'll always be a whore no matter what kind of handbag your mommy buys you. You'll always be a freak of nature. A rich little coke whore trying desperately to be a YUPPY.' I look up at the ceiling and hang up the phone, climb back into bed and cry.

Brett meets me on the limestone steps of the Pierpont Morgan Library. I'm early as always, living on sober time, which is about fifteen minutes to three days earlier than cocaine time. He's fifteen minutes late, red-faced and reeking of vanilla. Other than the vanilla emanating from every one of Brett's pores, it's every other winter afternoon, dark at five, filled with taxis, old newspapers, and rush hours that are longer than an hour.

'Why do you smell like vanilla?' I hug him, press my lips into his.

'I spent all day at the cake cafe testing frosting recipes. Since you've been gone, everything's changed in the art world. It's all about taste now.'

'As opposed to?'

'Never mind.' He takes my hand. 'Shall we?' He points up the steps and into the bronze revolving doors.

Cammie Greenberge is standing with his fat

blue-striped polyester back to me. I would have probably walked right by him, pretended I didn't remember him from the fifty-plus times I've been introduced to him, if I hadn't caught my father's name in his conversation. ''. . . Simon Woke's daughter.'

'The one who was pictured with him in the *Observer*?'

'No, that was his wife.' I stand right behind Cammie, just out of his line of sight. 'But his wife and his daughter went to high school together.'

'Sick. Those kind of sick people are really sick.' The clueless looking, mustached woman in Birkenstocks smiles, and all I can think is that maybe a thesaurus might be a good investment.

'Yes they are, really sick.' He nods.

'What about his daughter?'

'Well, she's really a piece of work.' I'm loving this, standing behind him, watching his arms flail around hopelessly trying to articulate his point, which is that I'm the anti-Christ.

'How do you mean?' The woman looks at Cammie. He's got a goatee, a little hair under his bottom lip; he looks sort of intellectual, like he once read a book and liked it. Though that's purely speculation.

'She's like this big slutty heroin addict, but worse than that, she's crazy and big. Really big for the daughter of a model. You'd think at the very least she'd be more attractive.'

'Yeah, why do children of famous people turn out that way?'

'Spoiled, self-obsessed, completely consumed with themselves, arrogant, useless, lazy.'

'Yeah.'

'I don't know. But watch out for her, 'cause she's not a nice girl.' He wags his finger at grey flannel jacket woman. She smiles and pushes her hips forward. Is it possible he's trying to pick her up by talking about how awful I am?

'Thank you for the tip, Cammie.' She laughs.

'She'll be here tonight. Though she'll probably be so out of it, that you won't be able to tell if she's even alive.' Cammie turns around. 'Oh, hi, Miranda.' It's a little too late in the social season of my life for etiquette to be an objective. 'We were just singing your praises, it's been so long, Miranda Woke.'

'I heard.'

He smiles awkwardly and disappears into a bathroom or a coatroom.

'This is why I get so paranoid.'

'It's kind of funny, isn't it?' Brett smiles with the knowledge that everything's become so absurd we can find the amusement in it, in each other.

'Perversely so,' I say.

We are at the party of Rolex, hair plug, yuppie men who are trying desperately to get to the models, who, in turn are being guarded by the rap stars and toilet paper heirs. Sober sight has shown me that being judged by your handbag and how much body fat you have is the height of stupid. And yet. I'm wearing the new Fendi baguette and liking it. I'm even getting a little contact high from stroking the big interlocking Fs.

Janice is supposedly on the board of this museum, a second home to youngish, richish, womenish women in pursuit of a husband. The MAM, the Madison Avenue Mafia, is in attendance. And so, as is to be expected, every single woman in the room is wearing the same matt black sheath dress cut right above the knee, slightly fitted around the waist, with either a black shawl or a black cardigan tied around her shoulders.

'Do you see Janice?' I say to Brett.

'No, nowhere.'

'Are you sure? You're not the best at looking for people.'

'Thanks. But no for the fifteenth time, I haven't seen her. Why do you want to see her? There's nothing to say, she's completely wacked anyway.'

'Not wacked, just confused. I mean I know she's a dope fiend, but maybe we could help her. She doesn't seem that bad.'

'Randa!' Brett rolls his eyes at me. 'How could she be worse?'

Other people's martinis start to look really attractive to me, they shine, sparkle, do everything short of actually singing to me. I feel myself sinking, I start to wonder, obsess about why everyone else in the world can drink and I can't. I feel very lonely in this big room filled with people, all of whom are communicating in the shared language of inebriation.

There is no sign of Janice or anyone else we know, so we leave. And in the cab I feel comfortable in the knowledge that we are both two rotund Jewish kids going back to my mother's dusty townhouse to not have sex.

Morning is an entirely new thing for me. I haven't had a morning since I was eleven and now here I am, citizen Woke, reading the newspaper, more accurately Page Six of the *Post*, which can hardly be called by anyone's definition a newspaper. I'm eating half a dry bagel, with a little butter mashed into it and drinking grainy coffee.

The doorbell rings and I get up, not thinking about who would show up on my doorstep at eight on a Sunday morning. I waltz to the Simon and Garfunkle on the radio, through the living room, in my long yellow cotton sobriety nightdress. I pull open the door and Janice sways in front of me.

She's got a black eye.

'Miranda!' she cries.

'What happened to you?'

'Long story. Are you going to invite me in or leave me here to bleed to death on your door step?' Well, with options like that . . .

'Who is it?' Brett calls from upstairs.

Neither of us responds. Some things don't change.

On the street, all these people are walking around in their Sunday J. Crew best.

'Janice!' Brett climbs down the stairs, and gives her a peck on the cheek. 'Come in.'

She walks into the living room, as though it's her own and sits on the sofa.

'How are you? I was worried. Where have you been?

'Where's the banker? What happened? Can I get you something?' I motion to the kitchen table, where there's orange juice and bagels

'A clean needle.'

'Come on, Janice.' Really, we've got juice, bagels, and there are a few doughnuts lying around here somewhere.

'A fucking clean needle, what good are you now?'

'Stop it.'

'Why? Don't you like seeing me this way? Come on, Randa, you get some kind of pleasure out of all this, don't you? I know you do.'

'No, I don't.' All my feelings feel fuzzy, inaccessible. 'I get no joy out of watching you suffer.'

'Shut up you little sanctimonious shit.' She leans back on my mother's sofa, lighting a cigarette. She smells. She's dirty. And she's high, so high I wonder if she will remember this.

I can see Brett start to lose it. First his face goes white, then his eyes get very wide, and then he starts to rush towards her, screaming.

'Get out, Janice, get the fuck out.' Brett grabs

her by the hair, but he's so much shorter than she is that he's destined to lose.

'Get off me, you fat fuck.' She pulls her hair out of his hands, stands up, shakes him off her and smacks him down on the sofa. 'Get the fuck off me.'

'What do you want?' I'm standing on the far corner of the room, looking at her and realizing for the first time that she might be more miserable than I ever gave her credit for.

'I just wanted to rest, see what's happened to me, see what Jon-the-banker did. See that? Look at me, look at my eye.' She walks over to me. Her eye is bad, bruised and swelling.

'Get her some ice,' I say to Brett. He disappears into the kitchen.

Janice and I are alone in the living room.

'Can I get you something to drink?' I ask her.

'Vodka tonic.'

'A little early.'

'Oh, I forget. Miss patron-fucking saint. Orange juice will suffice.'

'What do you want? I can't give you drugs because I don't have any, but anything else. Anything else you need,' I say to her, pouring the juice into a tumbler, looking back at her, at her black-and-blue wrists.

'Fuck you, Randa.'

'Don't say that to me.'

'Why the fuck not?'

'James called me last night. He's looking for you.'

'I don't give a shit. That's over.'

'He cares about you, you know.'

'Yeah, but I don't give a shit about him. I never have.'

'Stop! You're just in a bad state right now. You'll feel better later.' She downs the juice and rises from the sofa.

'I don't really need any of your therapy talk, thank you very much.'

'Are you gonna be alright? What happened to you anyway?'

'That banker, Atlantic City. I'll spare you the details.'

'So, are you going to be alright?'

Brett comes back in with ice. He looks at me and hands the ice to Janice.

'I just need a hundred, a hundred and twenty.'

'Fine.'

'Then will you leave?' Brett chimes in.

'Shut up, Brett. Don't say that to her.'

She heads for the door. I give her some money, about eighty dollars. 'Here, this is all I have.'

'Why are rich people so fucking cheap?' She takes the money, pulls it right out of my hand, and turns to the door. She doesn't look at me, not once.

'Will you be alright?'

'I'm like a cat.'

And she turns down the steps and onto the side of East Sixty-Fourth Street that's filled with bare trees, tooling down the street on broken heels, in a ripped dress.

I walk back inside and into the kitchen, where Brett is standing, staring into the pantry.

The phone rings. We stand in the kitchen and listen to it.

chapter fourteen

I've been up all night thinking about James, Jeff, Janice, and stupid Cammie Greenberge, who I've decided is the worst human being in the world and I hope that his polyester back catches fire on someone's cigarette. I've been hanging on the door of the refrigerator, inspecting four pints of Ben and Jerry's in the freezer.

This is how my night has gone so far: I take a bite of ice cream, put the container back, go upstairs, try to rest, come back downstairs, take another bite of ice cream, this time a different flavor, and then back up the stairs, all the while consumed with my hatred of Cammie.

Mom calls at five-thirty, when my sugar high is just peaking. 'Mom. That bracelet you call a watch doesn't seem to keep time very well, it's five-thirty in the morning.' I walk with the portable phone down to the kitchen to get some more ice cream.

'Ohhh, I'm sorry, darling. I just wanted to see how you are and to ask you one quick thing.' I narrowly avoid tripping on Poody, who is lying on the landing between the steps.

'I've been back for weeks but it was nice of you to think to call. Aren't you coming back today, anyway? Aren't you supposed to be on a plane right now?'

'Darling, that's what I wanted to talk about. Mommy has a little thing coming up, a little party at Les Deux Gamins and I was hoping you wouldn't mind terribly if I were to stay a little longer here in Europe?'

'It's fine. Do whatever you want to do.'

'Don't be mad, darling. Besides, Mary Post is there. She'll take care of you.' I take off the top of the Chunky Monkey and dig my spoon in.

'Fine. It's fine.' I say in a way that could only mean the opposite.

'Darling, would you like to come out here, just for a few days maybe?'

I choke on a large piece of frozen banana. 'I don't think so.'

'Think about it.'

'OK.'

'Send you a plane ticket, darling.'

'Bye.' I spit the piece of frozen banana in the sink. 'Mom?'

'What?'

'I really miss you.' The banana gets stuck in the drain and the garbage disposal that's below, the one that hasn't worked properly since I was ten.

'I know, darling. I know.'

'Aren't you going to say you miss me too? That's what a normal mother would say. A normal mother would say she missed her daughter. Any number of my previous shrinks would confirm this. Normal mothers say they miss their daughters. That's what they do.'

'Of course I miss you. Of course, you know that. Oh god the car's here. Send you a plane ticket darling. Send you a plane ticket. Bye, darling.'

'But, Mom—'

'What?' She sounds really annoyed.

'I really don't like to fly coach.'

'When have I ever asked that of you?' I toss the spoon into the sink.

I stand at the edge of the small square kitchen. The tiles that line the walls have little animals on them. Outside the window, the snow blows in circles around the garden. The sun starts to move up above the horizon. I wash the dishes as if I was doing something more important.

The soap is blue and it makes a lot of bubbles on the plates. The bubbles slide right off into the soapy water. I run my hand over each plate; the water out of the tap is very warm.

There's a cookbook leaning next to the sink. I open it – *106 Fat-Free Cake Recipes* – with the thought that I might cook something. A grocery list falls out of the book. I look at the handwriting; it looks like my own, but the date is from 1978, when I was two. I realize it's my father's handwriting. The grocery list is unextraordinary: eggs, milk, and everything usual. But I look at the list for a long time, like I could discover something about my father from what he used to eat.

I go back to the dishes, drying them with a blue dishrag, trying not to think, balancing a cigarette in one hand and a dish in the other. I finish with the dishes, stack them, leave them there on the butcher block counter.

I turn and open the refrigerator, for another round of sugar. I pull a box of doughnuts out. I put a chocolate doughnut down on a wet plate. I break it into halves and then into quarters. I take a bite. The frosting melts on my tongue. Chocolate frosting is really highly underrated.

I stand in silence in the yellow kitchen in the large white townhouse where I grew up – if you could call it that. I take another bite, this time more slowly, putting more doughnut into my mouth. Doughnuts taste better than screwdrivers.

I know Jeff probably never loved me. I know that now. But that doesn't mean I didn't love him. But, Jeff's been relegated to my memories, somewhere between summers with my father and the first time I met Janice, and even then I'll only miss him when I have the time, when my nostalgia doesn't interfere with my adult life. I don't know why it is that I can so easily forget. I should, if life were fair, be lying a few rows over from Jeff in that huge Jewish cemetery in Queens, the one you drive by to get to LaGuardia.

I remember reading somewhere that 1997 was a

ilabilit:

very bad, almost devastating, year for wines, it was certainly a bad year for me, mostly because of wine.

I carry a stack of paper-thin plates to the cabinet and drop one on the floor.

I try to pick up the shattered porcelain, but slice my hand on a piece of plate. I'm slightly surprised that even after all I've been through I can still cut myself so easily on a piece of a plate, and I can still bleed from such a dull shard.

I wipe the blood from my finger and the sleep from my eyes. The world is almost awake now. I glance at the clock; it flashes 5:45 A.M. If I leave now I'll make it to the six A.M. meeting on Seventy-First Street.

I grab my peach coat, ready for another day. But all these thoughts get lost in my struggle to open the door and maneuver down the steps. Because I'm off into the daylight. .'

Deep Blue Silence
PAMELA JOHNSON

Maddie is haunted by a silence that surrounds her mother.

Silence. We came to depend upon it, an extra element. Vital as air.

As an artist, Maddie explores the silence without using words. She begins to make work for a major exhibition but is distracted; she may be pregnant.

Maddie discovers she, too, can be secretive. As the new work progresses, pieced together from fragments of broken glass, Maddie delves into a silence spanning three generations.

Pamela Johnson is a writer, critic, curator and lecturer on contemporary visual culture. *Deep Blue Silence* is her second novel.

Praise for *Deep Blue Silence:*

'compelling reading . . . the novel looks at the complex sources of inspiration that inspire new work' *Liz Hoggard*

'An elegant novel' *Belfast Telegraph*

'The preoccupation with the work of art and confrontation with her mother's past . . . makes this an enjoyable read' *The Oxford Times*

SCEPTRE

The Dress Lodger

SHERI HOLMAN

'Quite Dickensian, in the best sense . . . This is one of those historical novels which has a passionate, angry feel to it, making it more than entertainment (though it is certainly entertaining)' *Margaret Forster*

'Sheri Holman writes with extraordinary assurance and style' *Miranda Seymour*

Fifteen-year-old Gustine is a prisoner of the beautiful blue dress she rents from her landlord. Followed at night through the black alleys of Sunderland by a malevolent old woman to prevent her escaping with the fantastical gown, Gustine entices the men who are attracted to it. Her only concern is to keep her fragile baby alive.

Surgeon Henry Chiver is a prisoner of his past. Implicated in a notorious Scottish murder case, he is attempting a new life with his loving fiancée, hindered only by a chronic shortage of licit cadavers for his anatomy class.

Doctor and dress lodger come together in the filthy East End of the city, itself held hostage by cholera. Gustine will assist the doctor with his need for bodies, if the doctor will help her – until Henry's greed and growing obsession with her child challenges her loyalty to him, and Gustine must turn to her mortal enemy in the battle for her baby's life.

'Sheri Holman's prose, tart, racy and sombre, will sing in your soul a long while' *Frank McCourt*, author of *Angela's Ashes*

Sheri Holman grew up in rural Virginia and now lives in Brooklyn, New York.

SCEPTRE

Melting

ANNA DAVIS

'Very cleverly constructed, sharp, witty and distinctive'
Livi Michael

Jason, Fran and Eileen move listlessly from city to city,
conning everyone they meet. They're slick and successful;
spinning stories, melting their victims down like wax in a
flame until they're good and soft, then slipping away with
whatever there is to take. For years they've been small-time.
Now they're ready to take on something bigger.

A chance meeting gives Jason the idea for a grand scam in
Cardiff's Tiger Bay, centring on a restaurant called The Melt.
The intended victims are young Welsh artist Owen Meredith
and his father, a high-kicking multimillionaire Tom Jones
fanatic.

The scammers have only each other to hold on to in their
self-created world where nothing is solid and real. But these
consummate actors are beginning to confuse fiction and
reality. Can they really trust each other?

Anna Davis grew up in Cardiff and studied in Manchester.
She now lives in London where she works for a literary
agency, but also teaches part-time on Manchester
University's MA in Novel Writing.

Her first novel, *The Dinner*, is also published by Sceptre:

'A stylish tale, told with sensitivity and relish' *Guardian*

'Anna Davis's debut is as sharp and sparkling as breaking
glass' *Jill Paton Walsh*

'A stunning off-the-shoulder debut in suicide red' *Attitude*

SCEPTRE

Swimming Sweet Arrow
MAUREEN GIBBON

A powerfully wrought, explicit tale of friendship, passion and survival.

Close friends since the days when they used to play truant to go swimming in Sweet Arrow Lake, at eighteen Vangie Raybuck and June Keel are girls out to have fun. And that means dope, booze and sex with their boyfriends Del and Ray, usually in the same car. After leaving school, they take the sort of dead-end jobs that are all rural Pennsylvania offers, Vangie sets up home with Del and June moves in with Ray and his brother. But while Vangie begins to realise there's more to life than sex with Del, especially when he's drunk, she sees June in danger of losing herself in the small-town life they'd sworn to escape and set on a course fated to end in tragedy.

Maureen Gibbon grew up in Pennsylvania and now lives in Minnesota. She is a graduate of the Iowa Writers' Workshop, and her short fiction and poetry, which has won several prizes, have been published in various literary quarterlies. *Swimming Sweet Arrow* is her first novel.

∫

SCEPTRE

colourbook
ROSALYN CHISSICK

'Of course a sister is going to love a brother. But there is something else. He can't find the word for it – an edginess that sits between them, it is like still air before the beating of wings, like the millisecond before an explosion.'

Against a loveless backdrop, Pia and her half-brother Luke grow up to form a passionate bond that leads them away from home and into a wild, hand-to-mouth existence. In spare yet emotionally charged prose, Rosalyn Chissick charts a relationship that challenges society's boundaries and conventions. A shocking, poignant and poetic novel by a prize-winning writer.

praise for colourbook

'Written in extremely accessible but very sparse prose, Rosalyn Chissick's second novel is as haunting, thrilling and memorable as her first . . . An unforgettable book' *Shine*

'Occasionally a novel is so absorbing that it makes your world stand still. Rosalyn Chissick's latest offering, *colourbook*, does just that' *Big Issue*

'*colourbook* is a work of some definite literary significance' *The Times*

Rosalyn Chissick is a novelist, poet and journalist, who lives in Somerset. Her first novel, *Catching Shellfish Between the Tides*, was published by Sceptre in 1998.

SCEPTRE

Cold Mountain
CHARLES FRAZIER

A soldier wounded in the Civil War, Inman turns his back on the carnage of the battlefield and begins the treacherous journey home to Cold Mountain, and to Ada, the woman he loved before the war began.

As Inman attempts to make his way across the mountains, through the devastated landscape of a soon-to-be-defeated South, Ada struggles to make a living from the land her once-wealthy father left when he died. Neither knows if the other is still alive.

'A beautiful book, written in exquisite prose' *Kate Atkinson*

'A remarkable first novel, a romance of love, of friendship, of family, of land. Frazier has inhaled the spirit of the age and breathes it into the reader's being' *Erica Wagner, The Times*

'A poetic account of hardship, violence and longing . . . From a simple framework of alternating narratives, Frazier builds up a richly detailed portrayal of a vanished world . . . The novel is above all a sustained flight of the imagination' *Daily Telegraph*

Charles Frazier has taught at universities in North Carolina and Colorado. He has published short stories and travel books, and lives in North Carolina with his wife, where they raise horses. *Cold Mountain* is his first novel.

SCEPTRE

A Vaudeville of Devils
ROBERT GIRARDI

'Seductive . . . Girardi, a skilled storyteller, writes sensuous prose that unapologetically invokes the supernatural' *The New York Times Book Review*

The highly-acclaimed novelist Robert Girardi creates seven unique worlds for his characters in this new collection of two novellas and five short stories.

In 'The Demons Tormenting Untersturmführer Hans Otto Graebner' an SS officer is made aware of mortality and morality by a degenerate artist. With 'The Dinner Party' Girardi gives us his own rich and peculiar version of hell on earth. 'Three Ravens on a Red Ground' portrays an American businessman faced with a Japanese take-over, comparing both cultures' versions of honour. Robert Girardi illustrates a world that is both beautifully alluring and brilliantly sinister, where souls are lost and won on the simple weight of everyday decisions.

'The stories in this volume are richly descriptive, with a whiff of the grotesque and macabre . . . Its inventiveness and brio suggest Girardi will soon be receiving recognition as an important writer' *The Times Literary Supplement*

Robert Girardi lives in Washington, D.C. with his wife and daughter. He was educated at Catholic schools in Europe and at the University of Virginia. He holds an MFA from the University of Iowa Writers' Workshop.

His previous novels, *Madeleine's Ghost*, *The Pirate's Daughter* and *Vaporetto 13* are all available from Sceptre.

∫

SCEPTRE

Bitter Sweet Symphony
SHYAMA PERERA

When Nina's husband abandons ship, her world collapses. But not for long: this is the here and now – we believe in life after love.

Bitter Sweet Symphony is Nina's story of modern love and triumph: of loss and laughter, despair and desire, men and menstruation, children and chance, vodka and vivacity. A vibrant tale of recovery and rediscovery, it's a battle cry for Woman Power: a call to pick ourselves up off the floor and party.

'The gut-wrenching shock, the humiliation and the terror of facing life alone are described with strength, wit and clarity. So is regeneration: the powerful consolation of friends and the revelation that life goes on' *Marie Claire, Book of the Month*

'Extremely readable . . . Written in an appealingly restrained, cool manner' *The Times*

'Perera writes with wit and panache about rejection. Chick lit at it very best' *Woman's Journal*

'A feisty variation on the lone and jilted theme, Shyama Perera's lament for lost love actually cheers you up' *She, Must-Read of the Month*

Shyama Perera was the first Sri Lankan child to be born in Moscow. Her mother brought her to England in 1962, in vain pursuit of her father. Now a writer and broadcaster, she lives in north-west London with her daughters, Nushy and Tushy. Her first novel, *Haven't Stopped Dancing Yet*, is available from Sceptre.

SCEPTRE

Self Portrait with Ghosts
KELLY DWYER

'Even jaded readers will be moved by this novel of quiet metamorphosis' *Publishers Weekly*

At the time of Luke's death, his sister Kate, an accomplished artist and sculptor, is working hard to rise to the demands of single motherhood and, at the same time, to forgive her sister's unspeakable disloyalty. For Kate's daughter, Audrey, Luke is a substitute for the father who left years earlier and has been barred from all communication with her.

With Luke suddenly dead, the entire family is prompted to re-examine the deceptions that tore it apart, as each member ultimately rediscovers what it is that makes life worth living.

Kelly Dwyer attended Oberlin College in Ohio and the University of Iowa Writers' Workshop, where she was awarded the James Michener/Paul Engie Fellowship. She was born and grew up in southern California and now lives in Oregon.